Large Print

TUR   Turnbull, Peter

        Treasure trove

Large Print

TUR   Turnbull, Peter

        Treasure trove

TREASURE TROVE

TREASURE TROVE

Peter Turnbull

Severn House Large Print
London & New York

This first large print edition published in Great Britain 2005 by
SEVERN HOUSE LARGE PRINT BOOKS LTD of
9-15 High Street, Sutton, Surrey, SM1 1DF.
First world regular print edition published 2003 by
Severn House Publishers, London and New York.
This first large print edition published in the USA 2005 by
SEVERN HOUSE PUBLISHERS INC., of
595 Madison Avenue, New York, NY 10022.

Copyright © 2003 by Peter Turnbull.

British Library Cataloguing in Publication Data

Turnbull, Peter, 1950 -
    Treasure trove. - Large print ed.
    1.   Hennessey, George (Fictitious character) - Fiction
    2.   Yellich, Somerled (Fictitious character) - Fiction
    3.   Police - England - Yorkshire - Fiction
    4.   Detective and mystery stories
    5.   Large type books
    I.   Title
    823.9'14 [F]

    ISBN 0-7278-7424-1

Printed and bound in Great Britain by
MPG Books Ltd, Bodmin, Cornwall.

To Fred and Paula Soutter,
whose splendid restaurant provided the
setting for this sinister story

One

... in which an ancient ruin is found to contain very fresh corpses.

TUESDAY, 13.10 HOURS – 17.27 HOURS

The old house had long held a fascination for Simon Knapp. He had first glimpsed it many years ago when just fifteen years of age and had stolen into the grounds to explore. His explorations rewarded him with the discovery of a large pond with a thriving carp and tench population which clearly had had only natural predators to contend with, such as the heron which Knapp often saw flying gracefully over the water. The banks were overgrown and there was a decayed boathouse with a crumbled jetty, because the pond was large enough – about the size of half a football field – and evidently deep enough to accommodate a small rowing boat. The discovery of the pond thrilled young Simon Knapp and he returned there the day after, small fishing rod and other tackle in hand and, keeping his own counsel, spent the happiest days of his adolescence fishing a rich pond which no one else knew about, and yet which was less than a mile from the rambling and hard-pressed housing estate where he lived with his rambling and hard-pressed family. On occasions, when he tired of lying on the tall grass beside the pond, watching dragon-flies hovering against the blue sky, he would leave his rod securely fastened and his keepnet also securely fastened, and would explore the grounds. With a realization and a power of observation that many would find remarkable when possessed by a fifteen-year-old boy, and especially so when Simon Knapp's home life would be deemed to have been 'under-stimulated', the young Knapp realized that what he was exploring was the grounds of a country estate which had been landscaped and which had then been 'returned to nature'. But not wholly to nature, for here were lines of beech trees – two lines perfectly parallel and two hundred yards long, between which was an open area of tall grass about fifty feet wide which once must have been closely cut lawn. The line of beech trees ran from the pond towards the house, which stood on higher ground, so that when standing at the pond, the observer looked up by raising his line of sight, but not his head, to the house. The beech trees gave on to an area of tall grass about, thought Knapp, the size of four football pitches, beyond which, upon a raised soil platform, was the house, by then a ruin. And with an insight, and an empathy, which would further have surprised many, given his age and difficult home circumstances, the young Simon Knapp realized that if one stood in the house, and looked out, then the pond would glisten tantalizingly in the distance. He would often leave the fishing, but for some reason never the pond, as if the pond represented some form of sanctuary, some form of home base; behind the beech trees was thick woodland, wondrously mystical, inviting and daunting at the same time, but clearly more daunting than inviting, because he never dared enter them. The walk between the line of beeches, through the tall grass, seemed, to him, to be giving too much to his own exposure, and the thought of walking across the vast, open area and up the incline to the equally vast house was, he found, so intimidating that he did not even contemplate it. The pond area, on the other hand, offered a familiarity, and from the pond a narrow path bent through a hedge, making a hole large enough for the spindly Simon Knapp to dart through. Beyond the railings was a stand of bushes; beyond that a main road which led directly home. It was for that reason that the young Simon Knapp remained near the pond, so that if his demons were realized and gamekeepers ran at him with their ferocious dogs, he could dash down the path, to home, and safety. The house, though, held a fascination for him and he would look upon it, whilst concealed from view, even though he was half a mile distant. It stood four-square, solidly built, a neat design with a clean roof line, similar to the roof line of Roman and Greek temples, and the pillars either side of the doorway suggested the same influence. Later in life, he was to find that his observations as to the style of the house were valid, for the architectural style was known as 'Augustan' and the building dated from the mid to late eighteenth century. The house's existence was no secret: it was boarded up and the entrance gates at the further side of the house, separated from the house by another generous parcel of land, were securely fastened, with large 'No Entry' notices hanging from them. Only the entrance to the grounds, via the rusted railings, close to the pond, was a secret, and it was a secret Simon Knapp kept to himself, and while he didn't force the railings, nor did he tread down the path through the grass which led to the pond. It was, he felt, the strangest thing that he never met anyone else when in the grounds: no other boys from the estate, no curious adult wandering the gardens, overgrown as they may be. It was only later in life that he realized the danger of wandering in such a place, when no one knew where he had gone, and where, if some mishap had befallen him – misadventure, natural causes, or murder – then his body would have lain undiscovered for decades, if discovered at all. But such thoughts no more entered his head than they would enter the head of any fifteen-year-old, and during those summer and autumn afternoons he spent by the pond, gazing at the old house in the distance, he felt he might have been the only teenage boy in the world. His life moved on, fishing no longer held the fascination it once held and, pressed and encouraged by teachers, if not his parents, Simon Knapp began to address his studies in earnest. He no longer crept into the grounds of Edgefield House, leaving it to other fifteen-year-olds to discover, and his life path took him away from York, to another similar city, but one in the south of England, and from that city to another city, and yet another, where he settled and bought property. He brought up three children and supported a plethora of animals, a Shetland pony for his daughters, a dog, and over the years many rabbits, hamsters, guinea pigs and goldfish, though he never allowed a bird in a cage to be in his house. Success followed success. His children's progress filled him with pride, and yet in his quieter moments the image of Edgefield House would flood into his mind. One day, realizing he had the time once again with which to indulge himself, he returned to Edgefield House, fifty years, almost, to the day since he had last walked out of the gardens.

He was to find the first dead body on the

main staircase, propped up, as if in some grotesque sitting position.

That day he felt the poignancy that many late-middle-aged persons feel when walking over childhood haunts. He walked the housing estate on which he had grown up, by then somewhat gentrified by superficial touches. The uniform drab green of each and every front and side door of each and every house on the estate had, for example, been changed to being painted yellow, blue, red and white in strict rotation. Simon Knapp could understand the reasoning behind the change but, himself, preferred the uniform green, not out of nostalgia but because he had found that the green doors, each behind a green privet and a small patch of lawn, made the estate very gentle on the eye, colour-wise at least. One or two tenants had chosen to exercise their right to buy their property and had boasted their owner-occupier status by having Georgian-style bay windows installed, which in Simon Knapp's view looked very silly indeed. Their owners had also chosen their own colour scheme which was at least an occasional and welcome break in the yellow, blue, red, white sequence. He walked the street on which his house stood ... his house ... 'our house' as it was always referred to fifty plus years ago ... now somebody else's tenancy. That pleased Simon Knapp. He had always disapproved of the policy of selling off public housing and was relieved to find that 'their house' was still owned by the City of York Department of Housing. He walked from their old house, further along their old street, to the edge of the estate and to the main road, beneath a row of mature horse chestnut trees. As he walked beneath one tree, a horse chestnut fell to the ground and exploded from its spiky green casing, rolling at his feet. He stooped to pick it up. It was large, large enough to have made a magnificent conker, but with the advancement of years his attitude had changed and he pocketed the nut. That particular nut would be rescued from the squirrels and the schoolboys and taken back to Manchester, potted, kept indoors and nourished for about three years, whereupon it would be taken to the Pennines and replanted with a protective cover. Simon Knapp had walked on. To an observer he would be a short, slightly built man, appropriately dressed for the weather in corduroy trousers, a pullover and a flat cap, and carrying a knapsack. He reached the foliage hiding the railings which boarded the grounds of Edgefield House and saw the path into the foliage was well trodden. He knew by that that the access to the estate had not been blocked off. It did indeed transpire to be as he remembered it: the rusted railings, bent and pushed aside, leaving a teenage-boy-size hole in them. He eased himself through the railings and walked to the pond and groaned with dismay. The pond was still there, still as large as he remembered it, and might even contain a few trout, but now the fish had to swim amongst old bicycle frames and old prams and much other non-biodegradable detritus. It had always been the same in Simon Knapp's experience, that once anything, in this case a lovely pond that would delight any angler, was despoiled by just one instance of fly-tipping, then it slid rapidly to ruin.

Simon Knapp skirted the pond but was unable to get near the water's edge because that area had become a receptacle for junk. Clearly, once the water had been filled, then leaving something near the water became the pattern. And all because the council charged a few pennies to collect unwanted metal. He had glanced along the open ground between the beeches. It was now dotted with young trees, too old to be called saplings and well established, though none yet appeared to him to be climbable. Beyond the beeches was the large open area, also now dotted with young trees, and beyond that, the building he had travelled to see – Edgefield House. Still much as he remembered it: those graceful Augustan lines, the columns by the door, sitting proudly upon the platform of raised earth. By then, fifty years since he had last seen it, he was no longer demonized by the thought of aggressive gamekeepers with ferocious dogs chasing him off the estate, and he walked towards the house. He was also protected by his excuse: he was a historian and the camera in his bag was for the purpose of photographing objects large or small which were of historical interest. The walk from the pond to the house took him a full forty-five minutes. The grounds were more expansive and the house larger than he had realized and once again, he felt himself alone as the mysticism of Edgefield House descended upon him.

He reached the house and, walking beneath it, he felt dwarfed by its grandeur. The reason for its decline was all too obvious, for, he realized, few could afford the upkeep of a property of this magnitude. He turned and looked back over the grounds and the pond and indeed, as he had once imagined it would, it glimmered appealingly and gently, tantalizingly in the distance. Without the pond in view he saw how the gardens would have been much less successful as an exercise in landscaping. He walked over a rough stone surface along what was the rear aspect of the house, dismayed by the graffiti, often obscene, sometimes naïve, of the 'Mary loves Jim' variety, sometimes just a pair of initials and a date, but never high-minded or humorous as with graffiti on the hidden walls inside the university. Simon Knapp walked round the side of the house and between the house itself and the remains of the outbuildings which were at the entrance of the walled kitchen garden. He found himself saddened by the relative narrowness of the house. It was long and thin, yet it still took him a full minute to walk at a normal pace from the back to the front of the house. The front of the house he found enthralling: it looked out on to wide grounds, now also tree-dotted, down a wide, straight drive which drove to two huge stone gateposts, perhaps quarter of a mile distant. The centrepiece of the front of the house was a curved stairway, which led up to the porch supported by four stone columns. As with the rear of the house, the walls at the front were heavily contaminated with graffiti; the wooden boards which covered the windows had been wholly or partially torn away, and where glass had been revealed, it had invariably been smashed. Simon Knapp walked to the steps, and then up them, one large step at a time, and when on the porch, saw intriguingly, invitingly, that one of the two huge doors was ajar. Only by a matter of inches, but ajar nonetheless. He paused and, knowing he probably shouldn't, turning round to check that no one was looking at him, and feeling like a sneak thief, he pushed against the door. It was heavy – it didn't move. He shouldered it until it gave, grudgingly, just sufficiently to enable his slender frame to slide through the gap.

The interior of the house was gloomy and musty but the boarding which had been torn from the windows allowed enough daylight to enable Simon Knapp to see all he needed to see. He saw that it all seemed solid – no dangerous holes in the floor, no massive crystal chandeliers set to free themselves from 200-year-old fastenings and come crashing downwards; the stairs seemed safe. All those rooms, all the cellarage ... the attic. Once in the house, the natural curiosity and the learned historian merged and rose together in Simon Knapp's mind, and the urge to explore became irresistible. He trod softly across the floor, and when halfway across the hallway, he turned to ascend the stairs.

His heart thumped in his chest; his stomach felt hollow. He gasped.

The body was that of an adult male. It was slumped on the stairway, in a sitting position, the body leaning against the plaster of the wall. It was a recent corpse ... by no means as ancient as the house ... the clothing was modern and the man was recently deceased, no more than a few days old, thought Simon Knapp. The features were clearly identifiable, but the flies told of the beginnings of putrefaction. He stared at the corpse, knew he should report his find, but did not. Instead, he continued to explore. He walked down the wide corridor which led off the hallway and had doors set along its length. Cautiously he opened each door and peered inside.

The shock of finding the second corpse was less than that of the first. That was a female corpse, also deceased by a few days, also in a sitting position, on the bare floorboards, leaning against the wall underneath the window sill. The third corpse came as no surprise at all – by then he had come to expect to find others – and the fourth had a sense of routine about it. Four corpses, four dead bodies, two male, two female, two apparently middle-aged, two apparently in their twenties. And that was only on the ground floor. The first corpse he had discovered seemed to him to be like a sentinel guarding the upper floor and the attic, and although there were other staircases in the house, Simon Knapp felt disinclined to use them. Four bodies was, he felt, quite sufficient for one day.

He walked back out of the house, down the wide, curved stairway and into the clear, late-autumn air. He looked about him. Nothing moved in the stillness; not a sound was to be heard, not even birdsong. Edge-field House had a sense of loneliness which held an appeal to him, though he doubted that that appeal would be universal. While he liked the tranquillity of the old house and its grounds, others, he fancied, would find it sinister and foreboding. He began to walk down the long drive, feeling small amid the enormity and the expanse. When he reached the gates, he turned and looked back at the house. The frontage of the house was, he thought, awesome in its grandeur and he felt a little surprised and disappointed in himself, that while he had spent the first twenty years of his life living only a mile from Edgefield House, this was the first time he had set eyes on the front of the house. He unslung his knapsack and plung-ed his hand inside and fished out his mobile phone. As he had grown older, he had more and more resisted change, but this particu-lar piece of modern technology he had reluctantly embraced. Selfish use of mobile phones in public places annoyed him, and the thought of his brain being microwaved frightened him, but his irritation and fear were more than counterbalanced by his family and friends being able to contact him easily and speedily and by, as on this occasion, his ability to summon the emergency services.

'At the gates of the entrance to Edgefield House,' he said calmly, though the female to whom he spoke seemed to be firing questions at him with a rapidity and aggression that he thought akin to the firing of a machine gun. 'And you'll need chain cutters...'

'Chain cutters!'

'The old gates are chained together, and haven't been opened for years.'

'How did you get in?'

'I crawled through a hole in the fence.'

'Wait there, a car is on its way ... but don't hang up ... stay on the line until the car arrives.'

'If you wish, though I can't tell you anything else.'

'Just keep the line open.'

Simon Knapp stood there, keeping the line open, looking at the passing traffic, the volume of which seemed to be growing as the rush hour approached. As he stood there one or two drivers and passengers glanced at him; a lone figure standing inside the old gates: evidently he represented a curiosity. The police car arrived with a rapidity that impressed Knapp ... it had clearly been in the area. He put the phone to the side of his head. 'The police are here now,' he said, and without a further word the operator cut the connection. 'Good day to you too, madam,' he added, speaking to himself as the two officers got out of the car and approached the gates. They both looked young, very young indeed.

'Mr Knapp?' The constable who spoke wore a very solemn expression. The second constable stood a little behind and to one side of the first.

'Yes.'

'There was a report of dead bodies?'

'Four. At least four, that I found.'

'Where?'

Knapp turned. He pointed to Edgefield House. 'In there.' He turned back to face the constables and patted the chain which held the gates together. 'I told the operator that you'd need bolt cutters ... mind you, it's well rusted, won't be any problem getting through.'

'How did you get in?'

'Through a hole in the fence at the other end of the grounds, about an hour's walk from here.'

'You could be prosecuted for that.'

'I dare say I could, and for going into the house as well but, going by the rubbish thrown into what was once a lovely trout pond, and the graffiti on the walls of the house ... well, it would be a bit petty to throw the book at me, especially since I have reported my find.'

'Well, that will be a decision for the inspector.' The constable took out his notebook. 'Can I take your name please?'

'Knapp. K.n.a.p.p. Simon.'

'Your age, Mr Knapp?'

'Sixty-five.'

'So, you're retired?'

'Yes, pleasingly ... this summer. I delivered my last lecture in May, well, my last lecture in my permanent-post capacity. I will still do a little teaching to keep my hand in, but I don't have to get up early each morning. Which explains why I am unconcerned about being prosecuted.'

'You're not immune from prosecution, Mr Knapp.' The constable's voice was stern, very stern indeed, and succeeded in stirring feelings of fear and respect in Knapp.

'I am not suggesting for a minute I am

immune, but being prosecuted at an earlier age may have cost me my job, depending on the offence ... but now I could murder somebody and get sentenced to life, but my pension will still be paid each month ... though I don't intend to be antisocial.'

'I am pleased to hear it, sir. Can I have your address?'

Knapp gave an address in Manchester.

'So, your occupation is that of teacher, retired?'

'I was a university teacher'

'At the University?'

'Alas not *the* University of Manchester, but at Manchester Trafford University. It's one of the new universities. It used to be Trafford College of Art and Design.'

'I see. Why did you come here?'

'Doing what you will do one day ... if you live long enough.'

The constable scowled.

'Well it's true, nobody's tomorrows are guaranteed. I was walking over childhood haunts. I grew up on the Broadwood Estate.'

'On the Broadwood!'

'Yes ... why, is it still as rough as it used to be despite all those gaily coloured front doors?'

'Rough enough ... keeps us busy.' The constable's manner seemed to have mellowed, as if impressed by someone who could survive the Broadwood and go on to make a good life.

'They're here.' The second constable spoke for the first time, and he and the first constable, and Simon Knapp, watched a police van approach and halt behind the police car. Officers in blue coveralls alighted from the van, one carrying a large pair of bolt cutters. Without being asked to do so, Simon Knapp stood back, well clear of the gates.

The officers holding the bolt cutters opened the jaws, placed them round one link of the chain and, with an ease which seemed to surprise all onlookers, cut the link in two. The officer placed the bolt cutters at a different place on the same link, compressed the jaws, the chain was severed and it was torn from the gates. The three officers from the van and the two constables from the car pushed against one of the gates. Simon Knapp, seeing no perceptible movement, despite great exertion from the five police officers, stepped forwards and pulled the gate. Being a small man, and in his mid-sixties, he knew his contribution was more token than actual, but he wanted to show willing, and importantly, his assistance was not rejected. Eventually, with a great creaking and groaning of tired metal, the huge gate began to give. First just an inch or two ... then a foot ... then finally the resistance of the rusted hinges and brackets vanished and the gate was opened wide enough to allow the passage of a motor vehicle.

'Don't know when they were last opened,' one of the constables growled, shaking rust dust from his coveralls.

'Always been shut since I have known them.' Another constable tested the second gate which was still in the closed position. 'And I grew up round here, remember these gates from my earliest days ... this one's fast, really stuck.'

'We've got one open.' The first constable gauged the width of the opening. 'That's all we need. Can you get into the car, please, Mr Knapp?'

The two police vehicles drove up the drive to Edgefield House and halted in front of the curved steps which led up to the front door, which the officer saw was slightly ajar.

'On the stairs, you said?' The driver of the police car turned to Knapp, who sat on the rear seat.

'Yes. You won't need me to show you.'

'You're not being invited to show us, Mr Knapp,' the constable snarled. 'Entering the grounds isn't trespass unless you commit damage, but going into the house ... that's unlawful entry. Despite contacting us, you could be charged, as I have said, depending what the owners say.'

'Be interesting to find out who does own it. It's been empty for an awful long time.' Knapp smiled at the serious-faced young constable. He still wasn't at all intimidated by the threat of prosecution for such a minor crime as unlawfully entering a dere-lict property.

'Four bodies?'

'Four ... one on the stairs ... three others in separate downstairs rooms. That I found. I didn't go upstairs or in the cellar.'

'Just wait in the car, please.'

Knapp watched from the rear seat of the police car as the five constables filed through the gap between the front door and the door frame, and then filed back out again within a matter of seconds. The driver of the car, the constable who had snarled at him and who had told him very curtly that he would not be invited to show them where the body was, walked to the police car, opened the boot and took out a spool of blue and white tape and returned to the house. He wound the tape round one column, tying it firmly in place, and threaded the tape round the other columns, so suspending it in front of the door. While one constable remained at the door, and Knapp felt for his loneliness, the two vehicles and the four other constables drove back to York, to Micklegate Bar Police Station, where Knapp was escorted into an interview room and asked to wait. He was not given an explanation and by then had learned not to expect one.

Later, he estimated that he had waited in the interview room for twenty minutes before a plain-clothes officer entered. Knapp saw he was tall, slender, neatly turned out, and estimated his age to be about thirty-five years.

'Mr Knapp?' the slender, youthful man asked.

'Yes.' Knapp noticed that the man carried a notepad and a larger statement pad.

'That's me.'

'DS Yellich.' Yellich sat in the vacant chair opposite Knapp. 'Quite a find you made.'

'Yes ... confess I wasn't expecting it. The officers didn't stay long in the building ... went in and out.'

'As procedure dictates, just sufficient to confirm a suspicious death. They didn't want to contaminate a crime scene, which is why we are a little disappointed you took it upon yourself to go walkabout. You should have left the house as soon as you saw the first body.'

'I see ... the other constable has told you what I said?'

'Yes ... but we'll have to go over it again–' he tapped the statement form – 'in the form of a statement which we'll be asking you to sign.'

'I would have thought you'd be better off looking over the house, I can be contacted any time.'

'That's being taken care of,' Yellich replied firmly. 'Just let us do our job. We're quite good at it.' He opened the statement pad and took out his ballpoint pen. 'So, you are Simon Knapp?'

'I am.'

'Four, sir.'

The flash of the Scenes of Crime Officer's camera jolted Hennessey's mind back to focus on the matter in hand. 'Four?'

'Bodies, sir.' The sergeant, clothed in white coveralls, stood next to Hennessey, though at a respectable distance. 'Four ... as we were told.'

'You've checked the whole building?'

'A rapid check, sir ... every room on both floors ... and the cellar. It was easy to do because the house has been completely cleared, as you see ... right down to the floorboards. But houses like this ... lots of little nooks and crannies ... I can't say every inch has been examined.'

'Understood.' Hennessey thought it a reasonable statement. 'We'll be doing that, of course.'

'Of course, sir. I'd like to take the covering off all the windows and do a fingertip of the entire building ... not enough daylight left today ... and we haven't even looked at the outbuildings yet.'

'Very well, thank you, Sergeant.' He turned his attention back to the forensic pathologist, who crouched back on her haunches, and by doing so, spoke of a lithe figure of excellent muscle tone which was concealed beneath the baggy green coveralls that she was wearing. He noticed her looking at the body which had been found in a near sitting position on the stairs, and doing so as if puzzled.

'Something wrong, Dr D'Acre?' Hennessey asked from where he stood at the foot of the stairs.

'Well ... wrong ... no.' Dr D'Acre glanced at him. She had short cropped hair and wore just a thin, almost imperceptible, trace of lipstick. 'But curious ... curious, yes.'

'Oh...?'

'Well, you know that you and I have a game...'

'A game? I'm sorry...'

D'Acre smiled but kept looking at the corpse. 'Yes, it's called "Let's Play That Record Again".'

'I'm sorry...' Hennessey had not known Dr D'Acre to be so obscure.

'Yes ... you know, it's the one where you say, "Can you pinpoint the time of death?" And I say, "That's a role that television police dramas have forced on us ... and it's become a case of life imitating art?"'

'Oh, yes ... and then you go on to say that the science of forensic pathology is confined, strictly speaking, to the how of the death ... not the when.'

'That's the one ... and then I go on further to say that simple observation is often as accurate as anything I can offer. He or she died somewhere between when they were last seen alive and when their body was found ... that is as accurate as any scientific findings I can offer.'

'Yes ... I know the game well. I don't doubt we will play it again.'

'Well, I mention it ... because I think that this man died at a different time from the other three corpses. The insect activity will tell us, but I think this man died a few days ago, the other three corpses seem to be of the same age but all are significantly older than this corpse. The significance of which is for your department ... and just the four corpses?'

'So far ... you probably heard the sergeant.'

'Yes ... nooks and crannies, as he said, may give up something, as may the outbuildings.' Dr D'Acre stood. Hennessey saw her as tall, statuesque. 'But four is sufficient, I would have thought.' She looked around her. 'Must have been a magnificent house once.'

'Sufficient, as you say. Any indication as to the cause of death?'

'What? Oh yes. Their necks have been broken. Snapped. Cleanly so. X-rays will confirm it, but I think that that will be the cause of death.'

'Snapped?'

'Yes ... snapped. I hesitate to call it a skill ... because it's destructive, it's the taking of life; but I understand the technique can only be learned. Anyone can kill by plunging a knife into someone, or pulling a trigger ... but not everyone can break someone's neck ... not deliberately anyway, and four corpses, all with their necks broken, speaks to me most strongly of a deliberate act.'

'Speaks most strongly to me of the same.' Hennessey glanced around him, constables and Scenes of Crime Officers, all in white coveralls, busied themselves in continuing the preliminary search of the ancient house. The flash of a camera bulb from one of the rooms off the main corridor told of one of the other corpses being photographed. He had to concede that the sergeant was correct: the house would take some time to

34

search properly. Days, in fact.

'Well, I am finished here.' Dr D'Acre closed her black Gladstone medical bag and stood. The late-afternoon sun shone rays through the stained-glass window at the turn of the stair, illuminating a myriad of flecks of dust hanging in the air around the forensic pathologist. 'If you have taken all the photographs, the bodies can be removed to York District Hospital. I will do the post-mortems tomorrow.' She glanced to her right and down the flight of stairs to where Hennessey stood. 'Well, they have been dead for a period of days ... and there are four. I need to be refreshed in order to do a good job.'

'Of course.' Hennessey smiled. 'Really, I wouldn't expect you to start four post-mortems at this hour of the working day, plenty for us to do ... though not one seems to have any identification ... no wallets ... no handbags ... no watches or other items of jewellery.'

'It's a puzzle all right ... you know, the way they have been left.' Dr D'Acre walked slowly down the stairs towards Hennessey and stood beside him. 'It's as though some-one wanted them to be found. There's a certain shock value in those poses ... the bodies have not been dumped ... yet someone has gone to a deal of trouble to conceal their identities.'

'That occurred to me ... we'll be paying a call on the university soon, I think.'

'The university?'

'A forensic psychologist ... we have used her before to good effect ... this sort of thing is right up her street. I'm sure we'll be picking her brains ... and ours as well. I mean, how on earth did they get in here? We had to force the gates to bring our vehicles in here. Those gates haven't been opened for years ... decades ... and this is the only vehicular access. The person who found them crawled into the grounds through a hole in the railings at the back of the house's grounds and it must have taken him a pleasant stroll to get from there to the house. Yet some person or persons unknown deposited four bodies here with sufficient time to place them in different rooms, positioned as if sitting ... at least propped up.'

'Persons...' Dr D'Acre glanced at Hennessey. 'One person could not carry these bodies to their final resting places alone, the males are large ... well-built ... heavy. If you were to place them on a stretcher ... I mean each one on a stretcher, and ask four men to lift them, one at each corner of the stretcher, then those four men would still have their work cut out to lift said stretcher, if those men were of average strength. Well, see for yourself ... he's a big man.'

Hennessey looked up the stairs to where the dead man was, propped in a sitting position, head forward and on one side. The man was indeed large ... larger than Hennessey had first realized ... his surroundings made the man seem small. 'Is the other man as large, in your estimation?'

'Oh, yes ... father and son, in my estimation ... possibly. Same height, so far as I can tell, similar facial characteristics.'

'And the women ... mother and daughter?' Hennessey gasped.

'Possibly ... again, same height and similar features ... allowing for age changes.'

'A family?'

'DNA tests will confirm that, but my guess is that you are looking at the murder of an entire family ... well, four members of the same family – it may be larger than just parents and two children, one of each sex ... but yes ... first impressions, of a professional eye with some years' experience, tell me that the four deceased are related, closely so.'

'Helps us at least...' Hennessey's eye was caught by the SOCO emerging from one of the rooms. The officer was young and looked unsteady on his feet.

'First corpse,' Dr D'Acre said softly, she too noticing the man. 'There has to be a first ... and the first is not necessarily the worst.'

'I'll say.'

She thought of a young woman she had once examined who had been hacked to death ... and George Hennessey's thoughts turned to a nine-year-old boy who had been run over by a laden juggernaut ... each of the wheels down one side of the vehicle had run over the boy, forcing the stomach and intestines to vacate via the anus.

'No telling where they were killed, of course.' D'Acre returned to the matter in hand. 'This is treading on your toes a little...'

'Oh please, tread all you like ... all help gratefully received.'

'Well, person or persons unknown would have to be persons if they were murdered elsewhere and their bodies carried here ... but if they had been lured here or coerced here ... then one person could have done it. The post mortem should indicate whether they were killed here or elsewhere. Will you be attending for the police, Chief Inspector?'

'Yes ... for this one, I will.'

'We'll start at nine a.m. sharp.' She smiled but avoided eye contact.

'I'll be there.'

'Eight thirty, for nine. I'll send the clothing to Wetherby, as soon as I remove it from each corpse.'

'Thanks ... that should tell us something.'

'Tells you they were not expecting to come here.'

'Oh...?'

'Treading again, but the men are in suits ... the women are smart, but casually dressed ... not the clothing I'd choose to wear if I was going to crawl through gaps in railings and access overgrown gardens to explore an ancient ruin. As I said, they were not expecting to make this visit.'

'They weren't, were they?'

'Nope ... but as I said, that's your department. I'll see you tomorrow, Chief Inspector.'

'Eight thirty, for nine.'

Hennessey waited for a few seconds, allowing Dr D'Acre to leave the building, then he too walked to the front door in time to watch her distinctive red and white Riley RMA *circa* 1947 drive slowly and sedately down the long drive. He thought how the classic car suited the scene, with its graceful lines and long running board, though the vehicle proved to be surprisingly cramped inside by modern standards. He waited until the car reached the gates and turned into the traffic stream and out of sight. He then walked down the outside steps, picked his way through the police vehicles and the gleaming black vans with 'H.M. Coroner' embossed in gold on the sides, and walked down the drive until he was halfway to the gate and then turned and looked back at Edgefield House and saw how it seemed to glow in the low, late-in-the-day, November sun.

'Those bodies,' he said to himself, 'those bodies have some connection with the house. More than just being found in there, more than that. Much more. That house has a history and those four are caught up in that history.'

It was Tuesday, 17.27 hours.

Two

*... in which Yellich discovers treasure
and Hennessey hears of a gentleman who
struggled to pay his tailor.*

WEDNESDAY, 09.00 HOURS – 18.15 HOURS

Louise D'Acre walked the length of the
pathology laboratory. She wore green paper
composite coveralls and a white paper hat
with an elasticated rim. The laboratory was
brightly, strongly illuminated by filament
bulbs whose glimmer was eliminated by
Perspex panels which formed the false
ceiling. George Hennessey, similarly clad,
stood silently at the edge of the room,
observing but certainly not participating, as
procedure dictated. Eric Filey, the short,
rotund mortuary assistant also stood in the
room, camera with flash attachment in
hand. Hennessey noticed that the man's

41

usual jovial nature, almost unique in one of his calling, in Hennessey's view, and thoroughly welcomed, was, that morning, absent. The four stainless-steel tables that stood in the pathology laboratory were each occupied, one deceased person on each, all lying face up, with a starched white towel draped over their coyly termed 'private parts'. Each corpse had been brought to the pathology laboratory, having stiffened with rigor mortis in a sitting position, and each corpse had had its rigor 'cracked' so as to enable it to be laid flat – laid in a metal drawer for overnight storage and laid on a stainless-steel table for cause of death to be determined. Having walked the length of the laboratory, Louise D'Acre stopped at the fourth and final table and turned to DCI Hennessey. 'Full house,' she said.

'Indeed.'

'Quite rare for this little city.' She pondered the corpse of the middle-aged man which lay on the fourth table. 'Our city has murders of quality, in my experience, but very rarely can it boast murders of quantity.'

'But in this case...' Hennessey raised an eyebrow.

'In this case, a murder of quantity. Four

souls despatched before their time. Necks broken, as I suspected.' She glanced at the X-ray display which showed four X-rays, each of a skull and upper chest. 'Snapped cleanly, as you saw.'

'As I saw,' Hennessey echoed. Though the actual fracture had had to be pointed out to his untrained eye.

'The cause of death is determined,' Dr D'Acre said matter-of-factly. She glanced at Hennessey. 'Dare say you'd like me to delve deeper?'

'As deeply as you can, Doctor. This is now a murder inquiry. Yesterday it was suspicious. Now it's a murder inquiry.'

'And an inquiry of some quantity.' She positioned the microphone, which was attached to a stainless-steel anglepoise arm, which in turn was attached to the ceiling, so that it was positioned just above and in front of her head. 'The first corpse,' she began, speaking for the benefit of the microphone, 'is that of a well-nourished male of about fifty to sixty years of age and approximately 183 cms or six feet in height ... white northern European by racial extraction. There are no marks or identification points such as tattoos on the anterior aspect ... I'll look at the posterior aspect in due course. The skin appears smooth ... the hands are soft ... the nails clean and well manicured.' She turned to Hennessey. 'He wasn't a working man. Mind you, we deduced that from his clothes, I caught sight of the Hathaway and Wynne label inside his jacket–' she smiled at Hennessey – 'tailors to the nobility and gentry since 1798' ... but the condition of the hands confirms that he wasn't accustomed to hard, manual labour. Probably would have foxed you if he was hard-skinned and had damaged nails in a suit made by Hathaway and Wynne.'

'Probably, but the charity shops are a great comfort to those who want to cut a dash but have little money ... I have a snout ... a grass...'

'An informer?'

'Yes ... uses charity shops to good effect that way, but I think this gentleman will prove to be the genuine article.'

'He certainly has the bearing, even in death ... there is selective breeding here ... taller, more appealing to the eye than the rest of us ... can't take it from them.'

'I wouldn't want to.'

'Neither would I ... it's very fragile bloodstock ... very prone to going wrong, like poor Toulouse Lautrec who gave us such lovely canvases of gay Paris when gay didn't mean what it means today.'

'Oh?'

'Yes, didn't you know?'

'I am familiar with his paintings.'

'He was born a cretin into an aristocratic family ... couldn't cut the aristocratic dash ... was shunned by his family ... went to live in a brothel in the Pigalle and stood on a wooden box and painted the social life he couldn't be part of. You can feel the pain of his rejection.'

'Can you?'

'The few I have met have always struck me as being very insecure ... terrified of their children not being perfectly formed, terrified of losing their status ... terrified of poverty, the pressure of sustaining their birthright.' Louise D'Acre shuddered. 'Rather them than me.'

'And me, happy in the hoi polloi, is I.'

'I am making a standard mid-line in-cision.' Dr D'Acre suddenly turned her attention to the post-mortem, clearly confi-dent about her audio-typist's ability to type the commentary only, and not the chat that interrupted it. She took a scalpel and drove an incision from the neck to the bottom of the ribcage, and from that point, two further incisions, one going down towards the left thigh, the other down to the right thigh, thus forming one large incision in the form of an inverted 'Y' on the chest of the deceased. She peeled the skin back along the lines of the incision, exposing the ribcage and the internal organs. 'Stomach is slightly distended,' she said, 'but that is not unusual for one of his years. When people talk about putting on weight, they really mean putting on gas. So let's see what he had for his last meal ... might help establish time of death. You may care to take a breath, gentlemen.' Dr D'Acre too, took a deep breath and turned her head away as she punctured the stomach with the scalpel. The gas trapped therein escaped with an audible hiss. She stepped back and waved the air with her arms in an attempt to disperse the odour. When the smell had dispersed, Dr D'Acre took the scalpel and widened the incision. 'Well ... well...'

'What have you found, Doctor?' Hennessey asked, taking a single involuntary step forward.

'Nothing...' But her tone of voice was serious.

'Nothing?'

'Yes ... well finding nothing, when you expect to find something, is always a source of surprise. You see his stomach is empty...' Mr Filey, can you take a photograph of this, please.' She stepped backwards as Eric Filey advanced with his camera. 'I think this will be relevant. If he didn't know hunger in his life, he certainly knew it at his death. It would take four days for a stomach to become as empty as this ... there are usually food remnants in the stomachs of people who haven't eaten for up to two days ... after that, the body starts to scavenge before it starts gobbling up the fat reserves.' She resumed her examination of the corpse once Eric Filey had returned to the corner of the laboratory. 'This man hadn't eaten for a number of days before he was murdered ... that wasn't self-inflicted ... nor was it by misadventure. The state of his clothing and the cleanliness of his body tells us that he wasn't trapped in the wilderness of the Dales without food before he was murdered. He'd have to have been kept against his will and deprived of food...' Dr D'Acre

turned her attention to the wrists and
ankles. 'There's no sign of abrasion which
might be caused by restraints. I would
expect to find them there ... or about the
neck–' she examined the throat of the
deceased – 'but none there either. Quite a
puzzle for you, Chief Inspector. But I dare
say that's what you are paid for,' she added
with a smile.

She turned to Eric Filey. 'I wonder if you
could help me, Mr Filey. I'd like the body
turned over, please. If you could take the
shoulders ... he'll be quite heavy ... we'll
rotate clockwise from your position ... on
three...' Dr D'Acre took hold of the feet and
said, 'One ... two ... three...' and the body of
the deceased was turned over with a
practised ease which Hennessey had wit-
nessed on other occasions, and which
always impressed him. 'There are no identifying marks on the posterior aspect of the
body,' Dr D'Acre said for the benefit of the
microphone, 'and no marks suggestive of
injury of any sort.' Dr D'Acre took the
scalpel and made an incision to the left of
the spine. 'I am examining the liver ... which
at first glance appears to be slightly en-
larged, but not grossly so ... tending to fatty

change, which is indicative of a regular drinker ... but it's a long way from developing fibrosis, which is the first stage of cirrhosis. He was a drinker in life, Chief Inspector ... a man who enjoyed his whisky at the golf club. He had been a steady drinker since his young days and would probably have enjoyed drinking for the rest of his life without succumbing to cirrhosis at all, or not until he was too elderly to care.' She carried the liver to the scales. 'One thousand eight hundred grams ... you see, just ten per cent above the median weight for a man of his build. He had hollow legs ... he would have been able to drink much without it having much effect on him.' She took the liver and placed it in a yellow plastic bag for disposal. 'Now–' she glanced at the body – 'the darkening of the buttocks ... it isn't injury ... neither is it identification marks, it's hypostasis.'

'Blood settling, due to gravity.' Hennessey had seen similar before.

'That's it ... and also on the soles of his feet. That's the blood in his lower legs ... once the heart stops beating, the blood remains liquid for a while ... a matter of hours in fact, and settles according to gravity. This man was found in a sitting position, and he died in that position. The hypostasis in the buttocks and the soles of the feet are utterly consistent with him dying in that position. It is safe to assume that he was alive when he entered the house. And that is body number one: death caused by a broken neck at the second vertebra; he enjoyed a high standard of living, but did not eat for a few days before he died; no signs of a struggle, no defence injuries ... no sign of being restrained or held against his will ... but what more can he tell us? Mr Filey ... can I have your assistance, please?' And once again, the heavy weight of the deceased male was rotated until it lay face up on the stainless-steel table. Eric Filey placed the standard white towel across the deceased's midriff and then retreated to the edge of the room, beside the scales, as Dr D'Acre advanced on the head. She took a stainless-steel rod, forced it between the teeth and prised the jaw open. They gave with a loud 'crack' which echoed round the pathology laboratory. 'Probably ought to have come here first,' she said, holding the jaw open. 'The mouth is a veritable gold mine ... plenty of recent dentistry, so his dentists will have records which will confirm his identity ... British dentistry too ... but that comes as no surprise if his tailor is in York. The tongue is distended ... filling the mouth. He wasn't just hungry when he died ... he was also thirsty ... very thirsty indeed. And thirst is never, ever self-inflicted. People will go on fasts but will never deprive themselves of fluid ... panic sets in if someone gets thirsty enough ... people will drink anything, just to get fluid down their throats. Contaminated water is just the beginning ... folk have been known to siphon petrol from their cars, just to be able to drink something, so crazed with thirst had they become.'

'Blimey!'

'Nothing else in his mouth of note, but that is sufficient ... good standard of dental care ... gold fillings ... and a very large, swollen tongue.' She turned to Hennessey. 'What's the betting that the other bodies will tell the same story?'

'I am not a betting man, but if I was, I'd say that it would be a safe bet.'

'I would say that too.' Dr D'Acre walked to the second table. 'The deceased is a middle-aged person of the female sex who was approximately five feet seven inches or 170 cms. She is white north-western European by racial extraction ... is well nourished ... with no visible injuries or identification marks...'

Three hours later the post-mortems were complete. Dr D'Acre found that all four deceased showed indications that they had been deprived of both food and liquid for approximately four days before they died, that the hypostasis pattern indicated that the deceased died where they were found, or that they were positioned there immediately after death. The latter, she added, was the most probable explanation. Their necks would have been broken, then their bodies would have been propped up against the wall, legs on the floor, or in the case of the older man, sat on the stairway. The body on the stairway died at a later date than the other three bodies ... the male body on the stairway could be described as 'fresh', in the first stage of decomposition; the other three bodies had reached the second stage of decomposition and had begun to bloat.

' 'Tis a puzzle,' Hennessey said at the conclusion of Dr D'Acre's preliminary, verbal report.

' 'Tis indeed–' Dr D'Acre allowed herself a brief smile at Hennessey – 'but one I am sure you are up to.'

Hennessey returned the smile. 'Thank you for that vote of confidence.'

'I'll fax my report to you as soon as it's typed up. It will be done today ... it'll be on your desk by tomorrow a.m. at the latest. But those are the nuts and bolts. The clothing has been bagged and tagged and sent to Wetherby .... DNA results will be back later in the week and I am confident that they will confirm that all four deceased belong to the same family ... mother, father, son and daughter. No grandchildren to worry about ... the daughter was sexually active, as is to be expected of one of her age, but had not given birth. So unless there are third and fourth and subsequent siblings out there then, as I said, no grandchildren.' She paused. 'There appears to be quite an age gap between the parents and children. The parents, if they are parents...'

'They will be.' Hennessey glanced at the corpses. 'You can see the son in the father and vice versa ... facial similarity is there all right. And it's there with the mother and daughter ... it's a family group ... but ...

sorry, you were saying?'

'I was saying there is quite an age gap ... not remarkable ... the parents seem to be in their sixties, the adult children seem to be in their twenties ... it's not an extreme age gap ... I don't think that there will be any younger siblings ... but there could easily be older siblings.'

It was 14.30 hours.

'Hole in the fencing, boss,' Yellich replied.

'That's the only thing of significance that you have found?'

'So far, yes, sir.'

George Hennessey had left the pathology laboratory of York District Hospital and had walked out of the medium-rise, slab-sided building, across York, walking the walls, being the quickest route across the medieval city, to Micklegate Bar, where the head of Harry Hotspur had been impaled following his execution for treason in 1403 as a warning to any who dared defy the monarch, and into Micklegate Bar Police Station. He had had no appetite. Observing four detailed post-mortems had robbed him of any desire to take lunch. He had checked his pigeon-hole and finding only circulars, read them quickly, kept one for filing and consigned the other two to the waste bin. He had then signed out again and exited the building by the rear 'Staff Only' door, got into his car and drove out to Edgefield House, which stood on the western edge of the city. He parked his car beside a police van, located DS Yellich and asked him if he had found anything of note.

'A hole in the fencing?' Hennessey repeated. 'Whereabouts? Not the same one the reporter found ... the one at the back of the house by the pond?'

'No, sir ... at the front by the main gate ... hidden by shrubs on both sides of the fencing and recently made.'

'Recently?'

'It appears to be so, yes, sir, as if jacked open. The railings seem to be bowed away from each other equally ... symmetrically I think is the word; clearly recently because of fresh scratchings on the rust, and also because vegetation appears to have been recently trampled. We've got a forensics team down there now.'

'Interesting.' Hennessey looked at Yellich. 'What does that tell you?'

'It's a possible source of entry, sir.'

'It's a certain source of entry, I'd say ... quite close to the house ... closer than the hole that's been torn in the railings by the pond ... but it should tell you something else.'

'Sir?'

'Well, I am thinking of the amount of graffiti on the walls of the house ... the broken windows ... and didn't the reporter mention, lament even, how the lovely trout pond he remembered has been filled up with rubbish? I think you mentioned that he did.'

'He did, yes, sir.'

'Well, it means the person or persons unknown who murdered the four people probably wasn't local, or he would have known about the existing hole in the fence.'

Yellich nodded. 'Fair point, sir ... well, they're probably not off the estate at least. I have the impression that the graffiti artists and the fly-tippers are off the estate. The Broadwood Council Estate is about a mile away, beyond the back of the grounds.'

'Ah ... take your point, Yellich. So, if the perpetrators are local, they are separated by class. What a lovely, class-ridden society we inhabit.'

'Lovely?'

'I was being facetious ... I've just learned to live with it and accept it ... doubt if I'll ever understand it.'

'I see, sir.'

'But you make a valid point ... the men had suits made by Hathaway and Wynne ... the two women had equally expensive clothing. The family, if it's a family, will have been missed already ... they will be well connected, very solidly, socially integrated ... powerful and privileged ... probably. If they were murdered by one of their social class ... that person would force an entry at the front of the grounds, not the rear.'

'It's also closer to the building, sir.' Yellich apologized for the devastating logic of his argument with a shrug of his shoulders.

Hennessey growled malcontentedly. 'Anything in the house?'

'Of note, of relevance to this inquiry, sir? Not that we have so far turned up, as I said, but there has been quite a treasure trove.'

'Oh, really?' Hennessey raised his eyebrows.

'Yes ... it's all in the life of a constable, the good, the bad, the interesting and the downright dull, but this day has proved fascinating for us ... exploring this old house room by room ... nothing in the cellars ... and I mean cellars, sir ... no little back-to-back-sized cellar here.' Yellich turned and stood sideways on to Hennessey. 'This cellar system ... well, it's what I imagine the catacombs to be like.'

Hennessey glanced at the dust and stains on Yellich's white coveralls. 'I see you've been down there.'

'Yes, sir ... no electricity, so we had to search the cellars by torch light. The boys started larking about, leaping out at each other ... but the sergeants growled at them.'

'I should think they did.' Hennessey was not impressed.

'Well, the cellars were thoroughly searched, sir ... nothing at all, they had been completely cleaned out. As had all the downstairs rooms ... as had the rooms on the first floor ... really cleaned out and we expected the same of the attic.'

'But not the case?'

'Not at all ... nearly though. There didn't appear to be anything at all in the attic ... we could walk over it ... it was fully covered with floorboards. About to give up when one of the constables ... in fact one of the ones who just an hour or so earlier had been larking about in the cellar, but by then clearly had his mind on his job, he saw something. A huge water tank ... looked to me like nineteenth-century plumbing. The house must have had its sanitation and running water modernized just as folk with pre-Second World War houses might have central heating installed.'

'Yes ... yes...'

'Behind the water tank ... as if hidden, there was a cabin trunk. We pulled it out ... it was a dead weight ... we forced it open and well, my, my ... you name it, it's in there ... small oil paintings, jewellery, silver ... a collection of Roman coins, all neatly labelled. We brought it downstairs ... if you'd like to see it, sir?'

'I'd love to ... be very interesting.'

'Not sure what to do with it, sir. I was going to ask your advice.'

'It's treasure trove,' Hennessey said. 'I'm sure it is. We can ask our legal advisers, but I'm fairly certain of the procedure...' The two officers walked towards the building. 'We'll have to declare it to the Coroner. He does more than order inquests, he accepts treasure trove on behalf of the Crown. He will have to ask an auction house to catalogue it and value it. We'll have to photograph and log each item.'

'It's in the house, sir.'

The treasure trove was just as Yellich had described it: first a solid cabin trunk – a constable stood sentinel beside it. He stiffened and stood back in a gesture of deference as Yellich and Hennessey approached. Yellich bent down and lifted the lid.

'Oh, my,' Hennessey gasped. The contents, to his untrained eye, did indeed appear to be valuable. 'Buried treasure,' he said. 'At least it's not been turned up by one of those appalling shell-suited scavengers with their metal detectors. Hidden rather than buried ... but nonetheless very interesting ... curious, as well.'

'Sir?'

'Well ... somebody must have known it was there ... that's the first point–' Hennessey ran a liver-spotted hand through his silver hair – 'and the second point is, how could a house be cleared out so thoroughly as this house has, yet a cabin trunk full of treasure be missed? It just doesn't add up.'

'Doesn't, does it?'

'Are you about finished in the house now?'

'About ... the boys are in the outbuildings now. A forensic team at the hole in the fence, as I mentioned ... there won't be enough daylight to do the grounds today, we'll have a look at that tomorrow.'

'Very good. You'd better ask the Coroner to send someone to take this into a safe place.' Hennessey pointed to the cabin trunk. 'Then get a police photographer and an officer to record each item ... the Coroner will have it professionally valued.'

'Yes, sir.'

'Then carry on here as long as you have daylight. You've already turned something up ... two things in fact ... never know what else might be out there.'

'Yes, sir ... can I ask where you will be?'

'Me ... I am going into the famous and faire,' he smiled. 'Going to see if the deceased paid his tailor.'

'Sir?'

'To Hathaway and Wynne's. It has to be the first lead as to the identity ... of the men, at least.'

Hathaway & Wynne's, established 1798, had premises in Colliergate. It had, Hennessey found, a narrow frontage, a small black-painted door with bay windows at either side, an upper floor which extended over the door, and an attic space above that. He opened the door, bowing his head so as to enter the shop as he did so, and was not at all surprised to see that the shop extended deeply into the line of the terrace. Long, thin floor areas were the pattern of buildings in the medieval part of the city, with a depth up to ten times the width of the frontage. The shop was quiet inside, very quiet, almost solemnly quiet. The deep-pile carpet absorbed the sound of Hennessey's footfall, cloth draped on finely crafted wood cabinets deadened other sound. The wood was dark-stained and highly polished.

'Good afternoon, sir. How may I help you?' The owner of the voice was a short man, immaculately dressed in a dark suit with a tape measure draped around his neck. He beamed at Hennessey.

'Police.' Hennessey flashed his ID and the beam disappeared.

'Oh ... no trouble, I hope?' The man's expression became serious – the beam was clearly reserved for paying customers. The more noble, the more gentrified, Hennessey thought, then the bigger the beam.

'Not for the shop, but trouble for others. I'd like to speak to Mr Hathaway or Mr Wynne.'

'Can't help you there, sir,' the man smiled as if enjoying a joke. 'I am afraid Mr Hathaway and Mr Wynne passed away a little while ago.'

'A little while?'

'About a hundred and fifty years ago, sir. Within a few months of each other. Mr Hathaway departed this world in his sleep and Mr Wynne was inconsolable and died of melancholy. So I understand. I wasn't with the firm then, sir.'

Hennessey, sharing the joke, returned the smile. 'Ah ... I would in that case like to talk to the present owner or the manager ... whoever is in charge.'

'That would be Mr Riddoch, sir. If you'd care to follow me?'

Hennessey was led up a flight of stairs and along the first floor, past shirtsleeved men who worked in silence, measuring and cutting cloth. As he passed they glanced at him with a haughty indifference. The floor, uneven with age, tilted first one way and then the other, giving Hennessey the impression that he was on board ship in a swell. His guide, on the other hand, clearly very familiar with the floor, anticipated each incline to the left or right and walked without faltering. At the end of the floor was a dark-stained door. The man halted in front of the door, waited for what Hennessey thought was a curiously long time and then knocked on the door twice, paused and then knocked twice again. There was another pause and then a voice from behind the door said, 'Come in, Mr Asty.'

Mr Asty opened the door wearing his beaming face and said, 'The police for you, Mr Riddoch.' Asty stood to one side, allowing Hennessey to enter the room. He found it small, cramped. He took his hat off and nodded to Mr Riddoch, also a small man, but more rotund and fuller-faced than the beaming Mr Asty.

'The police?' Riddoch glanced at Asty. 'Thank you, Mr Asty.'

Asty left the room, closing the door behind him.

'Please ... Mr...?'

'Hennessey, Detective Chief Inspector Hennessey. Micklegate Bar Police Station.'

'Mr Hennessey ... please sit down.'

Hennessey sat in the deeply upholstered

swivelling leather chair which stood in front of Riddoch's desk. The room was half-timbered – beams protruded from plaster-work. The small window behind Riddoch looked out onto a yard enclosed by ramb-ling medieval buildings. Large ringbinders lay piled on the floor besides Riddoch's desk, having spilled over from the available shelf space. Hennessey thought the office quite healthy in an emotional sense, being always chilled when confronted with a neat desk with not a pen out of place, the desk calendar and table lamp perfectly symmetri-cal ... but Riddoch's office pleased him, and he began to relax.

'How may I help you?'

'You are the managing director, Mr Rid-doch?'

'Yes. Owner and MD. My family bought the company some years ago ... we kept the name because of its status ... a bit like Volks-wagen kept the Rolls-Royce name when it took over the company.'

'Yes, I heard of the demise of Mr Hatha-way and Mr Wynne ... one inconsolable without the other.'

'It is the history of the company as handed down through the generations ... strange, but believed to be true. Most business partners that I have met hate each other like poison but not those two, if legend is to be trusted.'

'Seems not ... Well, I don't want to take up any more of your time than is necessary, Mr Riddoch, but I am hoping that you can identify two men ... both of whom were found deceased.'

'Deceased? I am sorry ... *two* men as well.'

There was the soft sound of a man walking towards the door. Then halting.

'Yes ... sadly. One was wearing a Hathaway and Wynne suit.'

There was a knock on the door. Three taps ... a pause, then a fourth tap.

'I see ... and you want to know if I can help you identify them?'

'Yes.'

'Come in, Mr Nuttall.'

The door opened and a young man, wearing a suit of the same dark colour as worn by Mr Asty, entered the room. 'Sorry to disturb you, sir, but you asked to see this as soon as it came in.' He handed Riddoch a sheet of paper.

'Thank you, Mr Nuttall.' Riddoch took the paper, glanced at it and laid it on one side as Mr Nuttall smoothly exited the office, closing the door with a gentle click.

'Sorry ... you were saying, Mr Hennessey?'

'Yes...' Hennessey put his hand into the inside pocket of his jacket and retrieved the envelope. 'These photographs were taken of the deceased in the mortuary.'

'Oh, my.' Riddoch fumbled for a pair of spectacles and located them under a sheet of paper.

Hennessey handed Riddoch two of the four photographs. 'The elder one was the person who was wearing one of the suits made by Hathaway and Wynne.'

'I see.' Riddoch held the photograph at arms length and moved it closer, seemingly until his eyes focused. 'Oh my ... oh my ... not often does a tailor look at such photographs. Oh my, indeed.'

'Do you recognize the gentlemen, sir ... either one or the other.'

Riddoch placed the photograph of the younger man on his desk but continued to hold and study the photograph of the elder man. 'I think I may ... but not for some time have I seen him if it is who I think it is ... not one of our wealthier customers.'

'I would have thought all your customers

were wealthy, Mr Riddoch.'

'There is wealth and wealth ... we have customers who have saved for years to buy one of our suits or sports jackets ... and take loving care of it. We have other customers who have a wardrobe containing twenty or thirty of our suits and another wardrobe containing the same number of sports jackets. This gentleman falls into the first category ... I think ... oh my ... on a slab ... it doesn't look like a slab.'

'It's a stainless-steel table in actuality.' Hennessey swivelled the chair. 'Folk still speak of the "mortuary slab" though.'

'Well ... time to pick brains, Mr Hennessey.' Mr Riddoch reached forward and picked up the telephone on his desk, an old Bakelite model with a dial and two intertwining cords leading from it to the wall socket. He dialled a two-figure number. 'Mr Fahy? Good. Can you come to my office for a moment please? Thank you.' He replaced the phone with a 'clunk' which made Hennessey yearn for earlier years when everyday objects did indeed seem to be heavier and more solid than in the present day. 'Mr Fahy will tell us, if he can. He's been with us many years and has measured girths as they have expanded with age and good living. I think I know who it is but would rather not say until Mr Fahy has given his opinion.'

Again, a soft footfall was heard approaching the door, again it halted for a distinct pause, then the knock. This time it was two taps ... a pause ... then three. After a pause in which Riddoch neither spoke nor moved, he said, 'Come in, Mr Fahy.'

Mr Fahy revealed himself to be a tall, slender man in his sixties, who in order to stand in Mr Riddoch's office had to bow his head.

'Mr Fahy–' Riddoch handed him the photographs – 'this gentleman is from the police, he wants to know if we can help him by identifying this deceased person ... he was apparently found wearing one of our suits.'

'Oh...!' Fahy seemed to Hennessey to be similarly stunned by the photograph. Such photographs were, as Riddoch had commented, clearly not a common event in a tailor's life. 'He looks different in death, if it is who I think it is ... I haven't seen him for many years.' Fahy turned to Hennessey. 'Is ... or was, this gentleman tall?'

'He was about six feet high ... or about one hundred and eighty-three centimetres.'

'I think it is Patrick Inngey.'

'Which is who I thought it was too, Mr Fahy.' Fahy handed the photograph back to Riddoch and left the office. Once again the door was closed with a gentle click.

'Very good tailor.' Riddoch nodded at the closed door. 'He retires soon, he'll be a loss when he goes. So, Patrick Inngey.' Riddoch swivelled in his chair and opened the drawer of a card file and fingered his way through the 'G's and the 'H's until he came to the 'I's, then slowed down and pulled out a card, leaving the card behind it protruding so as to mark its place in the drawer. 'Patrick Inngey,' he read, as Hennessey reached for his notepad and ballpoint, 'the Manor House, Long Hundred.'

Hennessey scribbled the name and address in his notepad. 'What do you know of Mr Inngey and his family?'

'Mr...?' Riddoch swivelled his chair back and replaced the card in the file index. Hennessey saw he wore a smug cat-that-got-the-cream smile. He turned his chair back to face Hennessey. 'Can't abide computers, dare say my son will introduce them when he sits here, but card indexes have a quality all their own. "Mr", did you say? Try "Lord"...'

'Lord!'

'Yes ... Lord Patrick Inngey. It is a hereditary peerage. Now pretty well a thing of the past, but he is of that era when they could still be inherited. Seems strange that until very recently we still lived in an age when mere birthright entitled you to a seat in the House of Lords and a part in the law-making process ... but I am a conservative ... I like tradition and dislike change. This company has thrived for centuries on the concept of trickle-down economics ... it has worked well for us ... and I am sure it will continue to do so.'

Hennessey remained silent.

'But what do I know of Lord Inngey? Well, I know he and Lady Inngey had known better times in life ... he had difficulty settling his last bill.'

Hennessey smiled.

'Something amusing in that, Chief Inspector?'

'Yes ... on a personal level. I assure you I am not smirking at the thought of a peer of the realm falling from grace with his bank manager. It is just that I made a joke, probably in poor taste, before I came here.'

'About paying his tailor?'

'Yes, in fact, it seems I have egg on my face.'

'Well, I don't know the origin of the belief that a gentleman never pays his tailor ... of course we get paid, promptly and handsomely, because our customers are gentlemen in every sense of the word. But Lord Inngey ... well, shall we say he struggled ... but he paid ... oh, he paid ... it will never be said in England that he did not.'

'I am sure–' Hennessey held up his hand – 'I did not mean to imply anything.' He was impressed at Riddoch's defence of his customer, intrigued too. It was not dissimilar, he felt, to a serf defending his master. He had a sense he was touching history, meeting a bygone social attitude. 'But, carry on, please...'

'Carry on?'

'Telling me what you know of Lord Inngey.'

'He had two sons...'

'Two?'

'Yes ... Mr Harold and Mr Percy ... both have accounts with us. Mr Harold is the elder by about ten years ... Mr Percy is the younger. Could I have a look at the second photograph?'

Hennessey handed Riddoch the photograph of the younger of the two men.

'Yes...' Riddoch studied the photograph, 'yes, that could indeed be Mr Percy.' He handed the photograph back to Hennessey. 'In fact that is young Mr Percy.'

'Thanks.' Hennessey placed the photograph back into the envelope and scribbled 'Percy – son' on his pad. 'Do you know anything else about his family? Wife? Daughter?'

'He mentioned his wife and daughter, yes ... never met them of course, they wouldn't come here any more than Lord Inngey would go into a ladies' hair salon ... I can't remember their names.'

'What was their source of income?'

'That I don't know, though I think it was limited.'

'They had the title but not the substance?'

'As, alas, is often the way of it these days ... the succession of socialist governments ... the welfare state ... all has to be paid for, the nanny state...'

Hennessey thought: Lucky for you if you

ever need a triple heart bypass operation –
but he kept his own counsel. He needed
Riddoch's co-operation.

'But yes ... the title but not the substance.'

'They lived as a family?'

'Yes.' Riddoch looked puzzled by the question.

'I mean the adult sons and daughter were
still at home?'

'Oh, that I could not tell you.'

'All right ... and you say you haven't seen
him for some time?'

'Lord Inngey?'

An urgent-sounding footfall approached
the door, halted, then knocked, tap ... pause
... tap, tap ... pause ... tap.

Riddoch waited for a few seconds then
said, 'Not now, Horace ... come back later.'
The footfall retreated. 'Tiresome boy. Now,
Lord Inngey ... no, I haven't seen him for a
few years ... pleased he was wearing one of
our suits, glad he didn't descend to the High
Street, that would be too bad for one of his
station.'

'Oh, too bad,' Hennessey echoed.

Mr Riddoch clearly being unable to help
any further, Hennessey thanked him and
took his leave. When he stepped out of the

74

low doorway of Hathaway & Wynne and into Colliergate it was to find that darkness had fallen quite suddenly, as it does in the autumn. He walked slowly amongst homeward-bound people through the narrow streets of low-level housing, feeling the chill of the east wind more deeply in his bones than in previous years ... age was wearying him, he thought, or this winter was going to be a bad one. He followed the Shambles into Pavement, into Ousegate, crossing the Ouse itself on Ouse Bridge, where new buildings blended with the ancient, up winding Bridge Street which became Micklegate, and to Micklegate Bar and the police station at the corner of the Bar, just beyond the traffic lights.

He signed in and walked down the CID corridor and, noticing Yellich at his desk, stopped at Yellich's office. 'How went the day?'

Yellich looked up and smiled. 'Went the day well, skipper, well, reasonably so. The Coroner said the treasure wasn't "treasure" in the legal sense as it was found in the house. So we'll need to wait to see who owns the house. Maybe it belongs to our four deceased.'

'By the name of Inngey.'

Yellich's jaw dropped. 'I see your day went well also, sir.'

'Quite well.' And Hennessey told Yellich about his visit to the premises of Hathaway & Wynne and his interview with Mr Riddoch therein.

'So, a name to check?'

'Yes. I'll ask the collator to do that now. But tomorrow, you and I will have to take a drive out to Long Hundred.'

'Very good, sir. Where is it?'

'Dunno,' Hennessey smiled. 'Bit of detective work to do for you there.' He raised his hand in a gesture of leave-taking and walked further down the corridor to his own office. He peeled off his coat and hung it with his hat on the hat stand and sat at his desk. He picked up the phone and jabbed a four-figure internal number.

'Collator.' The voice was brisk. Efficient-sounding.

'DCI Hennessey.'

'Yes, sir.'

'Got a name for you.'

'Yes, sir?'

'Titled to wit.'

'Not many of those, sir.' The voice was

heard to 'smile' down the phone.

'Lord Patrick Inngey, of the Manor House, Long Hundred.'

'Oh, Long Hundred.'

'You know it?' Hennessey heard a keyboard being tapped.

'Yes, sir ... it's out Malton way, this side of Malton. Nice country out there ... lot of farming money ... that's where you get Rolls-Royces in the car parks of pubs with thatched roofs. It's where the wife nips down to the shops in the Audi Quattro or the BMW when they've run out of teabags. I grew up in a village near there, but my dad was a farm labourer and when we ran out of teabags, I was sent to the post office shop on my bike.'

Hennessey grinned.

'Got a link with CR for you ... nothing about Lord Patrick but we have a Harold Inngey of that address ... his numbers would put him at thirty-five years of age as of this time.'

'Really? I thought we might have a missing person's report on a whole family, but not a link with Criminal Records. What does it say?'

'Harold Inngey ... he's got form for fraud

and embezzlement and GBH.'

'Grievous Bodily Harm ... really?'

'Yes ... convicted at York Crown Court of assaulting both parents, and an earlier conviction when he was about late twenties.'

'Sentence?'

'Six months for the first GBH and non-custodial for the second GBH. He went down for two years for the fraud and embezzlement.'

'Home address is the Manor House, Long Hundred?'

'Yes, sir.'

'Where the Rollers line up in the pub's car parks?'

'One and the same, sir.'

'All right. Can you send me up a print of that?'

'Yes, sir.'

'And cross-reference Harold Inngey to the case reference...' Hennessey twisted the file on the bodies discovered at Edgefield House which lay askew on his desk so that he could read the file reference number, which he then relayed to the collator. He put the phone down gently and glanced towards his office window, but it being dark outside, he saw only his reflection, the lined face ... the silver hair.

It was Wednesday, 18.15 hours.

Three

... in which the culture of a village is learned of, an angry woman is called upon and the good commander is gently assured.

THURSDAY, 09.00 HOURS – 13.00 HOURS

Hennessey and Yellich drove out of York to Long Hundred. A police vehicle containing two constables followed. There had been rain in the night. The atmosphere was still heavy with damp, the road surface still glistened, the fields of brown turned earth awaiting the winter wheat were sodden, the sky was low and grey but the rain had stopped and a dry day seemed to be promised. The two-vehicle convoy arrived at Long Hundred at approximately 9 a.m. and Yellich halted the car in the centre of the village. He and Hennessey looked about them. The village formed a 'V' shape with the point of the 'V' meeting at the duck pond, from which the line of buildings diverged round a large expanse of green. The buildings were rambling, two-storey, some white-painted plaster, others half-timbered – with the timbers clearly, in Hennessey's eye, aching for a coat of outdoor varnish or Bitumastic paint. No person was to be seen, no movement at all.

'Can't see anything which looks like a manor house,' Yellich smiled, tapping the steering wheel.

'Too early for the pub,' Hennessey grunted in appreciation of Yellich's humour. 'Try the post office. There must be a post office.'

'You'd think so...' Yellich looked about him. Behind them, the two constables in their vehicle waited patiently.

'There.' Hennessey pointed. 'This side of the road ... at the far end ... red sign.'

'I see it.' Yellich drove slowly down the left-hand line of buildings, followed by the police vehicle, and halted outside the post office. He got out of the car and walked to the building and pushed open the narrow green door. From the passenger seat of the car, Hennessey heard the jangle of the bell as Yellich opened the door. Yellich emerged a few moments later, giving Hennessey the 'thumbs up' sign as he did so.

'Follow our noses out of the village,' he said as he sat in the driver's seat. 'It's a large house on our left, clearly marked as the Manor House.' He drove off, slowly. 'There was something about her manner, boss.'

'Oh?'

'Yes, I think she figured me for a cop, but allowing for that, I think she was puzzled as to why I should want to go to the Manor House ... it was as if the house held some significance for the village.'

'Over and above it being the "big house" of the village? Every village has its manor house.'

'Yes ... that's what I mean.' Yellich looked to his left as the car emerged from the village and entered open country. 'Over and above that.'

'We'll see what we see.'

Yellich drove down the narrow road, muddy-surfaced, potholed in places and, he believed, in need of resurfacing. They cleared a stand of trees, still with the last vestiges of foliage upon them, and a house was exposed across a field from the road: low roof, tall chimneys, grey in colour.

Hennessey thought it looked forlorn. 'Ye olde Manor House,' he said.

Yellich took his eyes off the road for a second and followed Hennessey's gaze. 'Confess I was expecting something grander ... suits from Hathaway and Wynne's and all that. Mind you, he did say that my Lord did struggle to pay his bill ... and what else? Title without the substance ... but even allowing for that, I am disappointed if that is the Manor House of Long Hundred, Shire of York.' He halted by the entrance of a driveway. The driveway was unsurfaced and rutted, the wooden five-barred gate which once guarded its entrance now lay rotting in the open position, held on to the post by only one of the clearly original two hinges. A faded sign on the gate read 'Manor House'.

'I invite you to be disappointed, Sergeant Yellich.' Hennessey glanced at the sign, and the gate to which it was attached and the unsurfaced driveway. A murder of crows sat in the branches of the trees which lined the driveway, cawing loudly. 'And may I say that I share your disappointment.'

Yellich drove the police car slowly up the drive, trying as best he could to avoid the deep ruts, but he couldn't prevent the car bouncing and swaying until, eventually, he was able to halt it in front of the house.

The decay that greeted the officers at the entrance to the drive, with the rotting remnants of the gate and the rutted surface beyond the gate, was matched and mirrored by the house. 'Derelict' was a word which came to Hennessey's mind, and Yellich, more simply, thought 'ruin'. The house was low and squat, a ground floor and an upper storey, beneath a low-angled roof of grey slates, many of which were missing. The house seemed to have a plaster covering over its exterior walls, similar to one or two of the cottages in the village, but whereas many of the cottages had been lovingly whitewashed, the Manor House had been allowed to fade into a sickly grey colour. Above the door was a sundial, beneath which was the date AD 1649. Beyond the house was a series of wooden outbuildings, all of which seemed to be barely standing. Hennessey, taking in the vista with a sweep of his eyes, began to search for detail and, in doing so, focused on the front door. He thought it slightly out of true with the frame. 'The front door is open.'

'So it is.' Yellich saw what his senior officer

meant. The wooden door with metal studs on the outside was indeed very slightly ajar. 'Could mean anything, of course, village lads realizing the house is empty ... the son ... what's his name?'

'Harold.'

'Harold returning to search for something ... or the last person out didn't shut the door behind them.'

'I doubt the latter will be the case.'

'So do I, frankly, sir ... so do I.'

Hennessey and Yellich stepped out of the car and, following their lead, the two constables similarly exited the police vehicle. Hennessey turned and raised his voice sufficiently for it to carry across the distance between himself and them. 'Proceed with caution. We don't know what we are looking for, we don't know what we are going to find.'

'Very good, sir.' The senior constable nodded and raised his hand in a half-salute.

Hennessey turned to Yellich. 'Better announce our presence.'

Yellich took a deep breath and from his stomach, he projected, 'Hello ... Police...' He proved himself to have a powerful voice: his twin calls echoed in the stillness and caused the crows to take to the air.

There was no response from inside the house.

'We'll check the inside first ... then the grounds–' Hennessey walked slowly forward – 'but I think that this will be like your search of Edgefield House ... not done in a day.'

'Certainly not by us four at least,' Yellich smiled. 'And I doubt, like Edgefield, this house will have been stripped of its furnishings.'

'Doubt it too.' Hennessey approached the front door of the house and examined it. It was indeed ajar by a matter of only a few millimetres, but ajar nonetheless and the whitened, splintered wood told a story of its own. 'Forced entry,' he remarked.

'Forced entry?'

'Yes ... see for yourself, Yellich. So, as we agreed, this is not the last person out being absent-minded. Somebody got here before us.'

Hennessey pushed the ancient door open. It swung stiffly on its hinges and made a slight creaking sound. It was not often used, he felt that was plain. He called out a 'Hello?' as he stepped over the threshold.

His voice echoed in the building, loudly so, but elicited no response. He stepped into the entrance hall of the house, which was also clearly the living room. It was a room with a flagged stone floor, huge flags, each of which, Hennessey believed, could only have been lifted and laid by a team of men, possibly with the aid of a block and tackle. There was an old wooden table in the centre of the room, surrounded by four equally ancient upright chairs. Beyond the table was a stone hearth on which lay the embers of the last fire. Hewn wood, ready for burning, was stacked neatly next to the hearth. A smaller table stood by the window, which itself was grimy and allowed in only a proportion of the light it would have allowed in if it were cleaned, and at either side of the table stood two armchairs of the vintage which Hennessey guessed to be pre-Second World War. He recalled similar chairs from his childhood and even then they were considered old, and condemned as 'junk'.

On the far side of the room was a second, larger window looking out on to the overgrown rear garden containing items which had clearly been thrown out, an old mangle, a broken handloom, a decayed tin bath ...

books stood on the window ledge, all hard-back, two leather-bound. Curtains hung limply beside the window: the material seemed fragile, as if it would crumble to the touch. A Welsh dresser stood beside the window, containing an array of plates, and the drawers, Hennessey reasoned, would contain cutlery, table mats and similar. To the left-hand side of the hearth, a doorway led to a small kitchen. From his vantage point just inside the main doorway, Hennessey could make out a metal draining surface and an enamel sink. The air inside the house was musty and dampness gripped the chests of the officers as they stood in the room.

'And this—' Yellich breathed shallowly to reduce the damp of the house affecting his chest – 'this is the home of Lord Patrick Inngey ... Peer of the Realm. How the mighty fall. No wonder he had difficulty paying his tailor, if—'

'All right,' Hennessey cut him short, 'save all the comments until later ... Now ... we have to split into two pairs, we don't need to go room to room as a group of four. Yellich, you and one constable explore downstairs ... I and the second constable will take the upstairs.' Hennessey and the first constable walked towards the narrow flight of stairs which began beyond where the Welsh dresser stood, as Yellich and the second constable walked towards the small kitchen.

The stairs creaked under Hennessey's step, but he felt they were still sufficiently solid to take his weight. Hennessey sensed the constable clearly aware of his own weight, and began to ascend the stairs with extreme caution. The stairs turned back on themselves as they rose and led to a narrow corridor with rooms off. Hennessey pushed open the door of the first room he came to. It was a room of modest proportions, containing a single bed with its headboard up against the wall, while on a table beside the window stood a jug and bowl and an oil lamp. Hennessey glanced at the ceiling and then around the walls.

'No electricity,' he said. 'I didn't notice the absence of a light downstairs ... but the house is without mains electricity.'

'Yes, sir...' The constable peered into the room. 'It's like going back in time.'

'It is rather.' Hennessey continued to look at the room. He entered it and approached a solid oaken wardrobe and opened it by turning a small key and pulling a handle. It contained women's clothes and smelled strongly of mothballs. The clothing seemed to be contemporary, as if the owner had been content to lead a seventeenth-century lifestyle but her tastes in fashion were dictated by the times in which she lived. They left the room.

The next bedroom they entered was similar to the first. A single bed, a jug and bowl and an oil lamp. The wardrobe held male clothing, and like the clothing in the first bedroom, it was of contemporary fashion. Hennessey turned to the constable. 'Have a look under the bed, will you, please? Tell me if a chamber pot is there.'

The constable knelt on the threadbare carpet which covered the floorboards and peered under the bed. 'Yes, sir. And a few pairs of shoes.'

'All right, I won't ask you to look in it. I just knew it would be there. You're right ... this is what I believe writers of science fiction refer to as a "time warp". All right, next room.'

The third bedroom contained a four-poster bed. The room was larger than the previous two rooms and occupied a position at the end of the floor area of the upper storey, so that it had windows on three sides, the fourth side being given over to the doorway. Two wardrobes stood in the room. Before Hennessey opened them he knew it would be a 'his and hers' arrangement, and was proved correct. Similarly two chests of drawers stood in the room; atop of each were a jug and bowl and an oil lamp. A fourth room on the upper storey revealed itself to be a small bedroom, though unlike the other bedroom, the bed was stripped down to a hard-looking mattress, the wardrobe was empty and the jug and bowl covered in dust.

Hennessey and the constable joined Yellich and the second constable on the ground floor of the old house. Hennessey looked at Yellich and raised an eyebrow.

'Well, nothing obviously out of place or missing or damaged,' Yellich reported, used to Hennessey's method of asking for information. 'No damage at all, save the front door. The house is ancient ... it hasn't moved forward at all ... in fact only the enamel sink in the small kitchen seems to be out of kilter with the house and also a wood-burning stove ... Constable Pugh here tells me that the sink is early twentieth century and the stove is mid-nineteenth...'

'You know that, do you, Pugh?' Hennessey addressed the constable.

'Definite about the sink, sir,' Pugh answered confidently. 'The stove ... well, it's an informed guess.'

'Informed?'

'I took a degree in history, sir.'

'Ah ... I see ... and your opinion about the rest of the house?'

'It's fascinating, sir ... I think it's pretty well original mid-seventeenth century. No electricity.'

'Yes, we noticed.'

'The oil lamps are nineteenth century ... using paraffin of late ... not whale oil any more, as they would have done originally. We found some paraffin in bottles ... no running water ... the taps in the sink are not connected to anything, but there is a stand-pipe at the rear of the house.'

'You went outside?'

'Briefly, sir,' Yellich replied. 'Didn't explore the outbuildings.'

'I see.'

'Can't find a cellar,' Constable Pugh continued, 'I didn't think there would be one;

this is flat low-lying area and prone to flooding ... few houses in this area have cellars. The outside privy is an earth closet.'

'Really ... the frugal life, all right.'

'Seems so, sir ... A cold larder was used to store food.'

'A cold larder?'

'Stone shelving. Out of direct sunlight. Very cold in the winter, cool in the summer. Although the food was modern. The family were not above buying tinned food from the supermarket, but we haven't detected any means of transport. But, as Mr Yellich said, we didn't look in the outbuildings.'

'What's through there?' Hennessey pointed to a doorway set in the wall opposite the hearth.

'A study, sir ... a writing desk ... bookcases ... old books ... a hearth, again with embers of a recent fire ... only one armchair, as if it was the head of the household's den.'

'Might be worth a closer look then?'

'I'd say so, sir ... studies with personal papers therein have proved profitable before now.'

'Yes ... there remains the attic, of course ... didn't see a trapdoor.'

'It was above the top of the stairs, sir.' The

constable who had accompanied Hennessey spoke, as if keen to contribute.

'Good man.' Hennessey nodded in appreciation. 'I am declaring this a crime scene. Get SOCO here ... put a tape across the end of the drive and another across the front door. You see to that, Yellich.' He turned to the constable who had accompanied him to explore the upper storey. 'You and I will check the outbuildings.'

The man was not seen at first. Yellich and PC Pugh walked casually out of the house, Yellich reaching for his mobile to call for SOCO to attend, PC Pugh walking to the police vehicle to collect a spool of blue and white tape to cordon off the Manor House, as directed, yet neither saw him. Hennessey and PC Stanley, the second constable, also walked out of the Manor House, turning to their right to investigate the outbuildings, and had walked a few paces when their attention was caught by a man striking a match to light a pipe. Hennessey and Stanley stopped walking – 'We stopped in our tracks,' Stanley would later say – and Yellich and Pugh, hearing rather than seeing the match being struck, turned at the sound and they too stopped walking and looked towards the man.

The man smiled. He clearly enjoyed startling the police. He pulled casually on his pipe, lighting it on his own terms, at his own speed. He was dressed in an old dark-green sports jacket, an old grey pullover, dark corduroy trousers, heavy working boots caked in mud. His face was round and reddened as if from strong alcohol as much as from being weather-beaten. He wore an old felt hat, brown in colour, which sat seemingly very comfortably atop his head. A few silver hairs poked out beneath the hat. He carried a broken shotgun on his left arm. That he stood perfectly still against a brown and black background beneath a grey sky meant he was well-camouflaged even though standing out in the open. Hennessey realized that the man would have been seen eventually, but nonetheless he chose to announce his presence by striking a match. Yellich glanced at Hennessey, Hennessey responded to the glance with a nod and Yellich and Pugh went about their allotted tasks, whilst Hennessey and Stanley approached the man.

'Morning, sir.' Hennessey thought the man to be in his early, possibly mid-sixties.

'Morning.' The man pulled on his pipe. He was clearly a man of few words. He turned the shotgun so that both police officers could see that it was unloaded and then turned it back to its original position, holding it broken over his left forearm. 'And I have a licence. Wouldn't have let you see it otherwise.'

'And you are?'

'Styles. Arthur Styles.' He nodded at the ploughed field which lay beyond the forecourt of the Manor House. The boundary wasn't fenced. 'That's my land. Well, it's the land I have rented since I left the Army. I farm it and another few hundred acres ... close on two hundred and fifty ... arable mostly ... small herd of Herefords, but I work the land mostly.' He spoke with a thick Yorkshire accent and avoided eye contact. He had a serious attitude ... a dourness ... which seemed to speak of a hard life lived. A man who had struggled hard to make his rented acres pay.

'Can I ask your business?'

'I was coming to ask yours ... just saw yon car...' He pointed to the unmarked car in which Hennessey and Yellich had driven to the Manor House. 'Didn't see yon police

96

vehicle until I was a lot closer. Didn't recognize the car ... foreign ... I mean, foreign to the area. They're a strange family ... yon...' he nodded to the Manor House, 'but they're my neighbours ... so I saw the car, took a stroll over to find out what's going on.'

'You were out shooting?'

Arthur Styles patted the barrels of his shotgun. 'Aye ... haven't fired a shot yet ... a few magpies and crows ... there's too many of 'em, especially the magpies, their numbers have really risen. They take the eggs from the nests of other birds ... not a nice bird at the best of times and now there's too many of 'em. And the fox too ... there's a fox, really want him ... don't know where he lives, but he's not on my land otherwise I'd know ... but he got into my chicken run ... killed nearly twenty birds, then took the one he needed to feed himself and his little ones. That's what foxes do.' He continued to avoid eye contact.

'So you're neighbours.' Hennessey half-turned and indicated the Manor House. 'You said they were strange?'

'Aye...'

'In what way, would you say?'

'Why? Something happened to them?'

'Possibly.'

'Must have, really. Otherwise you would not be here, forcing your way in.'

'Well the door was open ... but if it wasn't we would have forced entry.'

'So something has happened to them?'

'Possibly ... well ... yes, it has.'

'Aye ... they were not dangerously strange ... just strange ... kept themselves to themselves. Hardly ever saw them, really, only knew they were alive because you'd see them in their old car ... or if there were lights burning at night.'

'We wondered if they had a car ... we found tins of food in the house with supermarket labels ... there isn't a supermarket in the village which is in walking distance, so we thought they must have a car.'

'Aye ... it's in one of the outbuildings. Well, if it's not been driven away ... it's an old Jaguar mark nine ... dates from the 1950s ... it's a mess of a car but it keeps going and manages to get its roadworthiness certificate each year. Mind you, we all know that's not worth much.' Styles continued to look at the ground, while pulling on his pipe. 'Anyway, they go out in it as a family and return in it as a family. Never seen the old man alone in the car, or just the old woman and the old man together. It's always all four, if the car moves at all. That's them ... just how they are.'

'Do you know the name ... the family name?'

Styles' lip curled into a smile – it was just the slightest trace of a sense of humour. 'Inngey is their name ... so they said ... reckoned they were Lord and Lady, but there's no truth in that.'

'Really?'

'Course not. I mean, look at the state of the house ... Lord and Lady indeed ... but they are mad as a family ... mad ... but harmless. So what if they want to pretend they've got titles, if it helps them get through ... what harm is there?'

'You ever had any dealings with them?' Out of the corner of his eye, he saw Constable Pugh walking back up the drive, towards the house, carrying a spool of tape. Clearly the blue and white tape had been strung across the entrance of the drive. Yellich also approached and said, 'SOCO's on their way, sir.'

'Dealings?' Styles coughed up phlegm and spat it out to his left. 'Not dealings like business, but I've said hello when I've seen them.'

'I see.' Hennessey turned to Yellich. 'Can you and Constable Pugh look at the out-houses, you might find a lovely old Jaguar. If it's there, it will tell us something ... if it's not, that will tell us something else.'

'Very good, sir,' Yellich replied as Pugh advanced on the door of the house in order to put a length of tape across the entrance.

'Nice to speak to ... had a posh accent ... had to speak like that if they were going to get away with all that Lord and Lady malarkey. They were a bit stuck-up ... would answer if you talked to them, but wouldn't speak first. But at least they'd talk to you ... Suppose you had to say that.'

'How long have they lived in the house?'

'For ever ... always been there. I grew up in the village. My dad ... least he said he was my dad ... but country living, it's not like towns, often a fella's name is put on the birth certificate just in order to prevent the lad or lassie being illegitimate. When I grew up I didn't look anything like my dad, but I was the spitting double of a labourer in another cottage that my mum kept talking to whenever they met. They're cousins in fact. But he was good to me ... even though I probably wasn't his, and I prefer being Styles ... it's the top family in the village. Mum's a Grunwell and the labourer who I grew up to look like is a Hodgin. They're both bottom families and don't have much pull. But the Styleses ... well, they've got the pub ... the post office ... and one of my half-brothers rents another farm. So we employ folk and when times are tight we look after our own.'

Hennessey thought that Long Hundred would not, despite the neat and well-ordered appearance, be a particularly pleasant village in which to live. The Manor House was inhabited by an isolated family who were probably insane, and the village population seemed rife with incest and nepotism.

'When did you last see the Inngeys?'

'Well...' Styles took the pipe from his mouth. 'Now ... to see them in the flesh ... a couple of weeks ago, they drove through the village in their old car ... last saw lights in their house last week. Have not seen light in their house since ... well, today's Thursday, must have been Tuesday or Wednesday of that week. Been a dark house all week.'

'Did you see anyone enter the house, or

even loiter outside it? Someone who wasn't a family member?'

'Or who was a family member?' The man's eyes twinkled.

'Meaning?'

'Saw Harold.'

'Harold Inngey?'

'Aye ... didn't recognize him at first. It was the walk more than anything ... very proper walk ... very erect. He was the firstborn and the only one that was sane. He left home as soon as he could ... joined the Royal Marines when he was eighteen.'

'The Marines?'

'Aye ... and stayed in for a good while, about ten years ... seemed to keep his nose clean, no trouble that I heard about, but was a bad lad after ... you'll know him.'

'Yes ... we do. So it was him you saw near the house? When would that be?'

'Few days ago. After the weekend. Monday or Tuesday of this week.'

'What was he doing?'

'Walking up and down the front of the house, looking at it.'

'Did you see him force the door?'

'I did not. I watched him from the far side of the field; he didn't notice me. I kept still, see. If you keep still people are less likely to see you.'

'So I noticed. You seemed to appear out of nowhere.'

'Aye ... it's a way I have about me,' Styles smiled. 'Can cause a real surprise, I can.'

'I bet.' It wasn't what Hennessey would regard as a positive attribute. He'd met such individuals before, people who enjoyed intimidating very weak personalities by creeping up on them. The ones he had met had seemed, by and large, to belong to the nether world of British society – the man who had never held a job who used the technique to intimidate his family was, in Hennessey's experience, of the type. He had never met a High Court judge or a surgeon who crept up on people, nor had he met a successful career criminal who did it. But small people, who upon their cremation occupied a larger space in the urn than they ever carved out for themselves in mortal life, were the manner of people Hennessey had met who would sneak up on people. They would also, in his experience, polish and hone the technique, seeing it, as Styles clearly saw it, as a skill; something to be proud of. 'So, Mr Harold Inngey did not break into the house?'

'Not when I saw him. He walked up and down the front, like I said, and then drove away. He knocked on the door and called out ... I saw and heard that, the field isn't that wide, as you can see. Close enough to see and hear ... so he was wanting to contact his family, got no response and left. Drove away in his red van.'

'He has a red van?'

'Red Transit ... that sort of van anyway, a thirty hundredweight, and red, bright red. Very distinctive. I'd have a chat with him if I were you.'

George Hennessey bit his tongue. Then he asked, 'Where do we find you if we need to talk to you again?'

'Day time, I'm on the land, somewhere on the farm or not far off it. Evenings, I'm in the Three Horseshoes, that's the only pub in the village. My brother is the landlord. Full brother, but he doesn't look like me; in fact, folk don't believe we are brothers.'

'A monopoly as well,' Hennessey commented.

'Monopoly?'

'Not only are you the top family...'

'One of the top families. The Pikes are big

round the village, but we don't have much to do with them.'

'One of the top families, and you also run the only pub.'

'Aye,' Styles smiled, 'we do. Folk have got to keep in with us or they have a long walk if they want a pint of beer and a game of darts of an evening. Well, I'll say goodbye.' Styles turned and walked back across the ploughed field, sliding cartridges into the barrels of his shotgun as he did so.

Hennessey turned away from the retreating, silent creeping Arthur Styles. Not a particularly pleasant character, just a product of the morally dubious-sounding culture of Long Hundred, but his information sounded promising, and the man was right: Harold Inngey had to be visited, for if nothing else, he still had to be informed of the death of his next of kin; something Hennessey decided that he would do. Yellich approached him.

'Just seems to be what you'd expect to find in the outhouses, skipper. The car's there, lovely Jaguar, don't make 'em like that any more. It's a bit of a wreck ... can't see it getting through many more roadworthiness tests.'

'So the Inngeys did not leave their house in their car. Yet they apparently went everywhere in it and went everywhere as a family ... bit of a weird bunch by all accounts.'

'Yet they died at different times, the adult children and the mother were older corpses than the father.'

'Exactly ... they were split up. It would take quite a force to do that, according to Styles.' Hennessey cast a glance over his shoulder. 'The Inngeys seemed to share an insanity as a family. I have come across such families before, sociologists call them "isolate" families, I believe.'

'I came across one once as well, skipper. The entire family was mad, made me think: Either I am insane, or they are.'

'Yes ... that's the sort of family the Inngeys are, aristocratic stock or not. You've seen their home and their car ... mad as hatters ... nutty as fruitcakes. The point is that three died at the same time, but something separated the father, and families like that don't get split up easily.'

'If they *were* split up, boss. It may be that the father was kept alive for a few days longer. If they were held against their will, it would be easy to separate them in that sense. Snap the necks of three, leave the fourth for a few days.'

'Yes, that might explain it. But the car is also significant. Styles told me they always went out as a family, all four, even if it was only a trip to the supermarket. So, if the car is here, it meant things went pear-shaped for them here. They were not abducted when they were out in their car. They were collected from the house.'

'Sinister.' Yellich pursed his lips. 'Very sinister.'

'We'll have to talk to Harold, the older son. You remain here and supervise SOCO and have a look in the loft.'

'Very good, boss.'

'I'll take Constable Pugh with me. I'll obtain Harold Inngey's last address from criminal records and take it from there.'

'Very good, skipper.'

'When you find him, let me know.' The woman was small. Less than five feet tall, so Hennessey guessed. She leaned on the frame of the door of a modest house. She wore a blue tracksuit, matching trainers, had dark hair cut short like a man. Late twenties, he thought, early thirties. A nice age ... youth and maturity combined.

'I'd Prefer you to answer the question, Miss...?'

'Hewlett.' She had a strong Yorkshire accent.

Miss Hewlett. He noticed hard eyes in the young woman.

'Miss Samantha Hewlett, "Sammy" for short. All right, no, he does not live here.'

'But you know him?'

'All too well. Do you want to come in? I don't like police officers standing at my door ... the neighbours round here are an awful lot ... this will give them something to gossip about.'

Samantha Hewlett lived in a neat semi-detached house in Dringhouses, two bedrooms and a boxroom and a bathroom upstairs, two rooms and a kitchen downstairs. Sufficient for a family, roomy for a single person. A small garden at the front, a larger garden at the rear, completed the home. The officers were invited into the back room of the house, clearly the living room: two armchairs, a settee, a bookcase, a television in the corner, a VCR beneath, a fitted carpet, all in dark but tasteful colours, a dark-blue carpet, dark television set, quite the opposite of the hideous chrome thing that had dominated the living room of a house recently visited by Hennessey, light-coloured wallpaper and light-blue curtains which reached the floor.

'Please, take a seat.' Samantha Hewlett indicated the chairs, while she sat in the armchair adjacent to the television. Hennessey sat in the facing armchair, whilst Constable Pugh sat on the settee, and remained silent throughout the interview, but noticing all he could; reading the room and listening intently to what Samantha Hewlett said, observing her gestures, her facial expression, her tone of voice.

'Can I help you?'

'Well, we'd really like to trace Harold Inngey.'

'So would I.'

'Why?'

'He owes me money. A lot of money.'

'Did he steal it from you?' Hennessey's eye was drawn to a framed photograph on the wall of Miss Hewlett in a martial arts suit.

'In a sense ... nothing I could go to you people about, but he tricked me ... but what he did was legal.'

'What did he do?'

'Got me to put up money to finance a business venture that just couldn't fail. If he had called his company "Titanic" it would have been apt. It sank very early in its life, and sank quickly.'

'I see.'

'I may look well set up to you–' she glanced round her room – 'but it's all on hire purchase or rented. I don't actually own very much and the house is heavily mortgaged. But before I met Inngey, I really was set up very well ... just twenty-eight, house all but paid off, full of my possessions.'

'You'd paid off all your mortgage at twenty-eight?'

'Sadly, yes.'

'Sadly?'

'My lovely father died suddenly ... younger than he should.'

'Natural causes?'

'Accident. He was painting his house and fell off the ladder. A neighbour found him. But I was his only child, he was a widower, I inherited everything, modest as it was. He held a lowly position in an insurance company, but his house was all paid off ... and he had cash in the bank. What I inherited enabled me to pay off my mortgage at the early age of twenty-eight, but I would prefer to have a father in my life, especially when he was such a lovely man. Very warm, very caring ... I felt very safe in his house when I was growing up. Country childhood as well. I had everything.'

'You grew up in the country?'

'Long Hundred.'

'The Inngeys' village?'

'Yes. I remember Harold and his brother and sister in the village. They didn't go to the village school like I did, went to boarding school, but Harold and I met in York ... we recognized each other, had a drink, agreed to meet at a later date ... one thing led to another and we became an item. He was very muscular. Ex-Royal Marine.'

'So we gathered.'

'Well, I like that in a man. I am attracted to it.'

'I see you are physical too?' Hennessey glanced at the photograph. 'What is your sport? Judo?'

'Well, that's one of me in a judo suit, but my sport is Thai kick-boxing ... different clothing for that, but I like that photograph.

I think it's a good one of me.'

'Are you employed?'

'No, I am between jobs. Which is why you find me at home at this time on a weekday. I have office skills, I am looking for work at the moment.'

'Are you looking for Harold Inngey too?'

'He won't be hard to find, he's still in York. Hasn't anywhere else to go ... he can't get a job. He's got form, you know.'

'We know.'

'Well, if he makes money, it will be as a self-employed person or as a criminal. He won't get a job, not one that's worth having anyway. It's not the GBH that is against him ... well, it is ... he really worked the guy over.'

'What happened?'

'Fight with a night-club bouncer, they don't usually take the second prize when it comes to a punch-up, but Harold-boy was not long out of the Marines and the bouncer was in hospital longer than Harold was in the slammer.'

'He got six months,' Hennessey gasped. 'It must have been some assault.'

'Out in three. Kept his nose clean, didn't he? But the bouncer was still in hospital when he came out. Then he got employment with the security firm that employed the bouncer, bit like the Army and the Ghurkas...'

'What do you mean?'

'Well, I read that in the nineteenth century the Army couldn't beat the Ghurkas, so they recruited them. "By Jove, we need these little fellas on our side" was one quote that I read ... it was a bit like that. The security firm thought they needed Harold on their side. Gave him a job and he worked for a few years, but his hand was in the till and he was back inside for a two stretch ... out in one...'

'He assaulted his parents,' Hennessey said. 'What do you know about that?'

Samantha Hewlett pulled her right foot up on to the chair and clasped her ankle. She did indeed appear to both Hennessey and Pugh to be very fit beneath the jeans and sweater. 'Well, I suppose you could say they escaped and I didn't. The nuts and bolts of that is that ... well, we were together as an item, he was living here ... this was his prison discharge address.'

'So you were together before he went to prison for the fraud and embezzlement from the security firm?'

'Yes.'

'You didn't break it off when he was arrested and charged?'

'Nope.' The answer was simple and clear.

'I see ... anyway, carry on.'

'Well he came out and moped about the house and he realized that if he was going to make something of himself, he was going to have to do it by enterprise, self-employment, and for that you need dosh. It's very difficult to start a business with nowt.'

'It has been done.'

'Aye ... but Harold wasn't too willing to be hard working and patient "labour and wait", that wasn't Harold's idea of doing things. Well, what do you know about the family?'

'Well we are getting to know more and more, but tell us what you think we should know.'

'I suppose you have found out they're titled? Harold's dad is Lord Inngey and his wife is Lady Inngey. When Harold's dad dies, Harold, the ex-con, will be the seventh Lord Inngey and any woman daft enough to marry him will become Lady Inngey. Hereditary peers can't sit in the House of

Lords any more ... thank heavens. Imagine a thug and a crook like Harold boy making our laws for us. It'd make you want to emigrate.'

'So, the assault on his parents?'

'Well, the story is that the family has a hoard of some kind, it's a rumour that has been passed down the generations, a treasure chest like you read in children's adventure books. Harold believed his parents knew where it was and that they were deliberately keeping it from him. One thing led to another and there was a fight. Their house had no telephone, but Percy, Harold's younger brother, had a mobile.'

'Ah ... I was going to ask.'

'He got fined very heavily for that, which put him in even worse trouble, but he was convinced that this hoard existed, and one day he dragged me to the family seat ... a ruin of a house ... it's Edgefield House ... a ruin of a stately home. The Inngeys lost the seat after one of Harold-boy's ancestors invested the family fortune in an Argentinian silver mine which allegedly produced silver of outstanding purity, and which transpired to exist only on paper.'

'A scam?'

'Of huge proportions ... the family lost everything. But the rumours of the chest of goodies continued and we went to the ruin one day, broke in and searched it from top to bottom. Stupid, I thought: who would leave a chest of treasure in a ruined house? But we went in every room. It was eerie but interesting ... and that's the other point: the house had been totally stripped, down to the bare floorboards, everything had been cleared out, there was no treasure there.'

'You searched the house?'

'From top to bottom.'

'Together, or did you split up?'

'Well, sort of both, really. There's a girl at the gym I go to, she told me that when she searches houses – she works in the social services and has to search houses where people have lived alone and have no known relatives – they occasionally come across money stuffed into shoeboxes, thousands of pounds, when the person had lived in poverty.'

'Yes ... it happens.'

'Well, she has to search these houses and does so with a colleague and they are told to imagine there is a rope about six feet long, tying them together. It's for their own protection in case a next of kin should appear and claim there was money or valuables in the house, then they can witness that nothing was found, but if they split up, there'd be no witness to say that any valuables were not found. If that girl was searching one room and her colleague another, one of them could find some jewellery and pocket it without the other knowing and that allegation could be made. But, if they stick to the rule about the invisible rope, then it prevents that allegation being made ... makes it more difficult at least. Anyway, we didn't keep as close together as that, sometimes we were out of sight of each other, and Harold-boy went into the cellar alone, I was not going down there.'

'You went in all the rooms?'

'And the attic. I was prepared to go in the attic. Harold split us up. I went one way, he went the other. There was nothing there ... just glanced in each section of the attic, it had been cleaned out. It was a complete waste of time but I did it to please Harold. He made a thorough search of his end of the attic. Me, I sat by an old cistern tank, kidding on I was searching, then after a while I went back to the stairs that led down from the attic. Harold was already there and asked me if I had found anything. So I told him the truth, I hadn't found anything. Well, I hadn't. He probably thought I'd searched in every nook and cranny like he had, but that would have been a complete waste of time. Harold wasn't best pleased and threw a tantrum and then said that it was at the Manor House. He said his father has something in the attic, behind a locked door. Said he was going to get it, one way or the other. That was four years ago. It was shortly after that that he persuaded me to remortgage my house to raise capital for his business venture that couldn't fail.'

'Which went down like the *Titanic*, quickly and when very new?'

'Yep.' Samantha Hewlett smiled a forced smile. 'Not bad, eh? But I wouldn't be so mad about it if it was my money ... but it was my father's, in a sense. His life's work went to finance Inngey's hare-brained scheme, which crashed in a matter of weeks, and I allowed it. But he's very forceful, very persuasive. He has the charm of a confidence trickster about him. So, when you find him, do let me know, because I would dearly like to Thai kick-box his face to pulp.'

'Where would we be likely to find him, in your opinion?' Hennessey asked.

'In my opinion ... well, you could try the security company he works for, Agar Security. It's on Agar Street, off Monkgate. He does a few shifts with them, moonlighting from his day job.'

'His day job?'

'He sub-contracts for a parcel delivery firm. He has his own red van, ex-Royal Mail. The parcel delivery firm often has too much stuff to carry, so they hire blokes like Harold-boy, who have their own vans, to convey the excess. "Percy's Parcels" they're called ... not owned by a fella called Percy but, like Agar Security, they call themselves after the street they're on ... Percy's Lane. I think it's off Walmgate somewhere.'

'We'll find it. Thanks.' Hennessey wrote both addresses in his notebook.

Once again, it appeared to George Hennessey that time had stood still, or it was an extended phase of déjà vu, or that he had been sent to hell and was condemned to re-live the same conversation with Commander Sharkey again and again. And again.

Responding to a note in his pigeonhole, he walked to the Commander's office and tapped on the door. He was greeted warmly and invited to sit.

'I don't want to issue a press release until we have contacted the next of kin, sir,' Hennessey said in response to Sharkey's first question.

'I see.' Sharkey was a slightly built man, for a police officer, probably even less than the minimum height requirement, but the board had been known to stretch the rules if a few centimetres stood between them and getting the candidate they wanted. 'But all members of the same family?'

'Definitely. An odd bunch by all accounts, lived a frugal existence in Long Hundred. It's a village near Malton. They were found on the other side of York in Edgefield House.'

'That's a ruin, isn't it?'

'Yes, sir. It can be seen from the road but the gates had been long closed before we forced them open yesterday.'

'Motive for the murder?'

'Well ... we don't know yet, but I'd like to talk to their son, the fifth and sole surviving member of the family. We have information that he believed his parents knew of a hoard of treasure.'

'Treasure?' Sharkey raised his eyebrows.

'Ancient heirlooms. The rich thing is that it exists. We found it. The son, Harold, entrusted the search of Edgefield House to his girlfriend, whose attitude was perfunctory at best. She actually sat within a few feet of it whilst killing time, in order to pretend to be searching.'

'Why Edgefield House?'

'It's the ancient seat of the family. The Inngeys are titled, hereditary peers, no less.' Hennessey smiled. 'Fallen from grace in a terrible manner, but we get a better class of customer in North Yorkshire.'

'Yes ... I don't like jokes, George.'

'Yes, sir.'

'George...' Sharkey paused. He glanced behind him, a little to his left and to a group photograph which hung on his office wall, showing him and fellow officers in the Royal Hong Kong Police Force. 'I dare say you know what I am going to say?'

'Corruption, sir.'

'Yes. I was only in that lot briefly. After I left the Army, they were recruiting ... Ex-Army officer was just what they needed, and the pay and conditions were attractive. I didn't realize the extent of the corruption. It wasn't like the British police force ... one bad apple now and again, and no pressure on him to be bent – they were all at it and I mean all ... and you didn't have to *do* anything. The sergeant would tell me not to patrol a certain area on a certain night, so I wouldn't, and the next morning there would be an envelope full of hard cash in my desk drawer. If I didn't take the money ... and worse still ... reported it ... well, I wouldn't be here now. I was only there for a few months, but I accepted the money, took it into my finances, used it towards our first house. So we have taken that money with us and will bequeath it to our children in the fullness of time.'

'I am certain that there is no corruption at Micklegate Bar, sir.' Hennessey was impressed by Sharkey's honesty, despite being irritated by his constant need to confess. 'I have my finger on the pulse of this building as much as anyone, and more than many; there isn't a bad apple here.'

Sharkey smiled. It was rare for him to smile. 'You can never be sure, you know that. It's the nature of the game ... the bad apple is often the last one you'd suspect. Anyway, you'll let me know if you have the slightest suspicions? I will pass it straight on to CIB3 for them to investigate ... but don't wait until you have proof. I want to hear any suspicion, any whisper.'

'Very good, sir. Understood.' Hennessey made to rise.

'Now, a minute more, George.' Sharkey held up his hand.

Hennessey sat. Heavily, as if in protest.

'About yourself, George. I have no complaints at all about your work, but you don't have long to go before you draw your pension. I don't want to put pressure on you when I should be taking it off you. I'll never forget what happened to poor John Taighe.'

'The maths teacher at your school.'

'Gave out all the signals: smoking like a chimney, big red nose, so he was hitting it in the evenings, overweight, way overweight, full of false good humour; could have made it to retirement, but they piled the pressure on. I only saw what happened with the full benefit of hindsight. He keeled with a massive coronary just a year or two before his last working day. Criminal. I often wonder what that will be like...'

'Having a heart attack!'

'No...' again a rare smile, 'walking out of your place of work, knowing that you have retired after a successful working life and with a pension ahead ... all that free time ahead of you and plenty of it, living to longevity as we do. You must let me know what it's like, George.'

'I will, sir ... and I do not feel under any more pressure than I can handle. I'd rather be out there. I don't want to police a desk, or work in traffic or guide children across the road.'

Hennessey left Sharkey's office and wrote up the visit to the Manor House in Long Hundred, the information provided by Arthur Styles, and also the interview with Samantha Hewlett. He added that the next stage in the inquiry would be to locate and interview Harold Inngey. Putting on his coat, he left Micklegate Bar Police Station, and walked the walls to Lendal Bridge. The day had turned blustery – the clouds seemed to threaten rain. Few tourists seemed to be on the walls; the majority of wall-walkers seemed to be, like him, local, knowing that the best way to get across the small city was to walk the walls.

He lunched at the Starre Inne on Stonegate, accessed by a snickelway into a small courtyard, wherein he relished a lunch of Cumberland sausage, chips and beans, smothered in a thick onion gravy as he sat beneath a facsimile of an old print dated 1610, of the 'Countie of Yorkshyre, ye famous and faire Citie York defcribed'.

It was Thursday, 13.00 hours.

Four

... in which an arrest is made and Detective Chief Inspector Hennessey is 'at home' to the gracious reader.

THURSDAY, 13.00 HOURS – 23.00 HOURS

Hennessey feeling refreshed, replete and satisfied by his lunch, left the Starre Inne to walk back to Micklegate Bar. A fine rain had started to fall, and as he left the snickelway to turn into Stonegate, he put his coat collar up and walked steadily on the glistening, slippery pavement. He took the pavement back to the police station – the walls might well be the speediest way to traverse the city for resident and tourist alike, but they are rapidly deserted in the event of rain. There seemed to Hennessey to be no logical reason for this. The walls are only a few metres above pavement level, two persons, one on the wall and the other below on the pavement, could hold a conversation with voices only slightly raised. With that modest difference in elevation, the rain would be just as cold and the wind just as biting whether on the walls or on the pavement, but the pavement just seemed to offer more shelter, and Hennessey, like the rest of the citizens and tourists that dull Thursday lunchtime, avoided the walls.

He entered Micklegate Bar Police Station, peeling off his raincoat as he did so, signed in, checked his pigeonhole and found nothing of pressing importance. He walked down the CID corridor and, passing Yellich's office, noticed the Detective Sergeant at his desk. He stood in the doorframe of Yellich's office. 'How went it?'

'It went very well, skipper. Just writing it up now. Hope to get to the canteen before the food runs out.'

'Don't know how you can cope with that gruel.'

'It's very cheap–' Yellich smiled – 'that helps it go down quite well.'

'Do you mind if I...?' Hennessey pointed to the chair in front of Yellich's desk.

'Please do, boss.'

Hennessey walked into Yellich's office and sat in the vacant chair. He noticed Yellich had a framed photograph of his wife and child on his desk. It was a recent addition to the clutter of Yellich's desk top. He thought it a welcome addition, and a good photograph as well – it captured the warmth of personality of both mother and son – though he didn't comment.

'Nothing of interest in the house, but when we looked in the attic...'

'More treasure?'

'Nothing either, but it was obvious someone had been there. The attic is divided into a series of sections ... each section had a locked door.'

'Had?'

Yellich smiled. 'Had. All the doors, about four of them, had been forced, splintered open at the hinges.'

'The hinges?'

'Yes ... not the locks. Someone knew that the easiest way to kick an old door open is to attack the hinges, not the lock, or perhaps it was just common sense. The wooden door frames were spongy to the touch. That house can't be rescued...'

'Cast a speculative eye over it, did you?'

Hennessey too smiled.

'Well, yes, actually.'

Both men laughed softly.

'It's a natural thing to do. While the SOCO were squirrelling about taking photographs, I stood back to avoid getting in the way. Just couldn't help my thoughts turning to wondering how much it would cost to fix up. It seemed solid on the ground and first floor, but just then SOCO called me up to the attic where they found the damaged doors ... saw the extent of the rot in the roof and lost all interest in the house. Only fantasizing anyway. I'd love an old house, but Sara wouldn't ever agree.'

'Anything in the attic?'

'No, cleared out. Either there was never anything there in the first place, or whatever was there had been removed, but I tend to think the former.'

'Why?'

'Well ... the doors had been kicked from their hinges, then forced open, so that leverage was applied to the lock, and the gap that seemed to be forced between the frame and the door would only permit the passage of one person. If something was removed, it would be something that could be pocketed.

I mean, the doors would have to be taken down completely to remove anything like the chest of goodies we found at Edgefield House.'

'So somebody was looking for something, somebody forced the door ... the front door, then went to the attic, then forced each door in the attic. Any sign of the house itself being searched?'

'None, sir.'

'Yes, it was all quite undisturbed, wasn't it? It could have been fleetingly scanned, or the person knew that if what he wanted was in the house at all, then it would have to be in the attic.'

'Seems a fair assumption.'

'And the person who forced the doors in the attic clearly didn't know where the keys were kept?'

'If there were any keys at all, boss.' Yellich leaned forward, resting his elbows on his desk top. 'Those locks were very old. I mean seriously old, as old as the building, which Constable Pugh noted was very old indeed. What did he say, mid-seventeenth century? So it was built when Milton was writing, that's old enough. But the rooms inside the attic were empty, nothing was in them at all.

It was probably cleared before the Inngeys took possession, but it's strange that they didn't accumulate any junk in the years that they were in the house.'

'That's strange ... nor did they force the doors in the attic, if they were locked when they moved in, which is the first thing that any homeowner would have done, I would have thought.'

'I would have thought, as well, but the Inngeys clearly were not any homeowner. A strange family, by all accounts. I read your recording, boss.' Yellich tapped the file. 'Going everywhere together by car, even it if was only to the supermarket.'

'Any other observations?'

'Neat. Very neat.'

'What was?'

'The break-in, the forcing of the doors in the attic, no more force than was necessary.'

'I see.'

'And the attic door, the trapdoor to the attic from the hall, was closed.'

'It was, wasn't it? I remember now ... so the person who broke into the attic, and forced all the doors therein, closed the attic door behind him. Never known any house-breaker do that before. Very courteous of him. A neat and courteous housebreaker, not many of them. So after lunch ... after your lunch ... mine is pleasantly settling, or should I say settling pleasantly? The latter, I think. After you have canteened yourself into another few hours of survival...'

'Yes, boss?'

'You and I are going to hunt down Harold Inngey.'

'We are?'

'We are. I want to have a few words with him.'

'You suspect him, boss?' Yellich's voice had a note of alarm. 'Parents, sister and brother?'

'The family is insane.' Hennessey stood. 'All those generations of inbreeding ... and he had money troubles.'

'So I read.' Again Yellich patted the file.

'So, let's find him, break the news of the death of his next of kin, his reaction will tell us much. Let's continue, step by step, see where we get to. Will you be ready by two thirty p.m?'

The man was large, very large, very muscular, and black. An Afro-Caribbean gentleman with a European hairstyle and dress

and, Hennessey and Yellich found, manner-
isms and accent.

'Yeah ... Harold Inngey.' He leaned back
in the chair causing it to creak. Hennessey
thought his bulk far too large for his office,
or his office far too small for his bulk. Either
way, he looked to Hennessey to be in des-
perate need of larger premises. 'He does a
few shifts for us.'

'Surprised you hired him. I understood he
put one of your men in hospital.'

'Well, wouldn't normally, but there was a
bit of a hidden agenda there.' The room was
stuffy. The windows grimy, but they let in
sufficient light for both Hennessey and
Yellich to see that the indifferent rainfall at
lunchtime had developed into a strong and
relentless downpour.

'Meaning?'

'Bad blood between them. There was
more to it than one of my guys ejecting a
badly behaved customer and taking the
second prize. Exactly what the bad blood
was, I don't know, but they both kept quiet
about it.'

'Something we should know about?' Hennessey glanced round the room, papers Blu-
tacked to the wall, calendars decorated with

133

scantily clad females.

'Probably. Can't see them wanting to keep it quiet for any other reason. Anyway, Inngey proved he could handle himself. We needed staff, he got the job. He works part-time. Lends a hand when we are short-staffed.'

'I understood security firms are careful not to employ criminals, especially those with convictions for violence.'

'We are, we ask people to declare all convictions.' The man smiled. The nameplate in front of his desk read 'Leonard Scall'. It was the name he gave when Hennessey and Yellich had introduced themselves.

'But don't check up on them?'

Scall shrugged. 'We do if need be. If they prove a management problem, we use undeclared convictions as a means of getting rid ... but if they are good at their job, well, we don't enquire too closely.'

'How did Inngey get in? You knew he had a conviction for grievous bodily harm, he worked one of your own employees over.'

'By invitation. We offered him a job. He worked for us, did all right, about eighteen months separated the fight from the court case, so when he came he still didn't have any convictions. When he came out of the slammer, he picked up where he left off. A few shifts here and there. Good man. He has a charm about him ... he's fairly classy.'

'So we gather.'

'He can use that to cool situations. Other guys we have had tend to feed critical situations, make them worse, but Harold can calm the situation. He has that way about him. I'd like him to work full-time.'

'I'd? It was "we" a minute ago.'

'We ... I ... we'd, I'd like him to work full-time.'

'What else does he do?'

'Drives a delivery van. I think he likes it, out on the road, better than standing outside pubs and night-clubs waiting for something to happen.' Scall leaned forward and interlinked his fingers, all heavy with rings. 'I think he wants better for himself. He thinks bigger than being a man with a van and a part-time doorman ... he wants more from life than that.'

'So, where can we find him?'

'All I have is his mobile number.'

'That'll do.'

Leaving Scall's office, Hennessey and Yelich stood in the doorway, sheltering from the rain, while Yellich rang the number provided by Scall. He got a voicemail. He glanced at Hennessey.

'Don't leave a message,' Hennessey said. 'Better be discreet. Let's go and talk to the man with the vans. What's their address?'

Yellich switched off his mobile and pocketed it. He took his notebook from his pocket, turned a few pages ... 'Percy's Parcels.' Yellich smiled. 'Could have thought of a better name, I would have thought. Sounds to me like a barrier to marketing, like a company that doesn't take itself seriously.'

'Well, they clearly survive, let's go and talk to them ... Percy's Lane, where away?'

'Wet route or dry route, sir?'

'Yes, there are times when a car would be useful, even in this small city. Probably should have listened to you, Yellich.' He glanced up. 'In fact I *should* have listened to you, this has set in for the day.'

'Well, the quickest way would be to follow Foss Bank into Foss Islands Road ... not much shelter ... bit exposed, though the town would offer more shelter, all those overhanging buildings.'

Hennessey pulled his hat down on his

head and turned his collar up. 'Lead on ... through the town.'

Hennessey and Yellich walked through the centre of medieval York, side by side when possible, but mostly in single file, as they joined other citizens who walked single file close to the buildings, making use of what shelter the architecture provided. Those people with umbrellas seemed to stand away from the buildings, allowing those without to make use of any projecting buildings. From Monk Bar and the beginning of ancient York, on their walk they followed Goodramgate into Colliergate, into Fossgate, and into Walmgate, behind which was Percy's Lane and the premises of 'Percy's Parcels'. Hennessey and Yellich stood outside the door as Hennessey pressed the intercom.

'Hello...' The female voice was crackly.

'Police.' Hennessey put his mouth close to the microphone. 'We want to talk to the manager.' And feeling water trickling down his neck and squelching inside his shoes, he added, 'Please,' with as much passion as he believed circumstances would permit. The door clicked open. The officers pushed the door back. It led to a flight of concrete stairs. At the top of the stairs was an office where a worried-looking young woman sat behind a small modern-looking desk.

'Police?' Her voice quaked.

'Yes, pet,' Hennessey smiled. He wondered whether she had something serious to hide or whether she just had a guilty conscience, of the sort caused because she once stole some money from her mother's purse when she was six years old. 'We would like to talk to the manager.'

The young woman stood and walked to a door opposite the doorway in which Hennessey and Yellich stood. She tapped on it nervously. A male voice said, 'What is it?'

The woman pushed open the door. 'Police, Mr Parsloe.'

'The police!' Parsloe's voice seemed alarmed. 'Ask them to come through.'

'Please come this way.' The nervous young woman turned to Hennessey and Yellich. 'This is Mr Parsloe, the Managing Director.'

'And owner.' Parsloe stood as Hennessey and Yellich entered his office and as the timid secretary withdrew. 'No trouble, I hope?'

'Plenty,' Hennessey said. 'Plenty of

trouble, always more than we can cope with, but nothing you should worry about.'

'I am relieved. Please take a seat.' Parsloe indicated two vacant chairs in front of his desk. Hennessey and Yellich sat. Hennessey 'read' the man, then the office. The man was short, slightly built, and 'dapper', he thought, might be an apt description. He wore a grey suit, red tie, short, dark hair kept short. He wore a wedding band. His office was neatly kept, an everything-in-its-place office ... neat desk top, just one lonely-looking plant atop the filing cabinet. The calendar, in contrast to Scall's calendar, showed the Aysgarth Falls on a pleasant, clear, autumn day, with the Falls themselves full-bodied as after rain. The window of his office, also unlike Scall's office window, was clean and looked out on to a yard and covered workshop beyond, where a single mechanic was working on the engine of a white van which had 'Percy's Parcels' written on the side in bold, glaring scarlet. Hennessey realized he had seen the vans of 'Percy's Parcels' many times, darting speed-ily along the roads in and around York, but only then did he connect them with the 'Percy's Parcels' mentioned by Samantha

'Sammy' Hewlett. So this is their home, he thought. A road map of the UK , which was pinned to the wall behind Parsloe, suggested nationwide deliveries.

'How may I help you?' Parsloe smiled as he glanced at Hennessey, then Yellich, then again at Hennessey, seeing him as the older and the more senior of the two officers.

'I'm DCI Hennessey and this is DS Yellich of Micklegate Bar Police Station.'

'Yes ... Victorian, red-brick building...'

'The very same.'

'So, how can I be of help?'

'I understand you employ a gentleman by the name of Inngey?' Hennessey flexed his toes in saturated socks.

'Nope.' Parsloe smiled a warm, knowing smile.

'I am sorry, but I was given to understand you do, or did?'

'Neither.' Parsloe continued to smile. 'We subcontract to him.'

'Ah ... yes ... that is in fact what we were told. My mistake.'

'He has a van, both he and his machine are reliable. I have more work than my fleet can handle, so we subcontract the excess to Inngey and one or two others like him.'

'We'd really like to talk to him, it is a matter of urgency.'

'I see. I can let you have his mobile phone number.'

'We have it, it's connected to his voice-mail. We have to press ahead, we can't wait for him to contact us.'

'Is he working at the moment?' Yellich asked.

'Not for me he isn't, not today. He might be working for himself. He puts notices in newsagents' shop windows – 'MAN WITH A VAN FOR HIRE' – and picks up work like that, but he hasn't been subcontracted any deliveries for us for a few days. Quite a few days in fact.'

'Really?'

'Yes, really. We deliver far and wide: Wales, Scotland, Ireland sometimes.'

'But Mr Inngey hasn't driven for you for some weeks?'

'Some weeks, that makes it sound longer than it is. About two weeks, no more than that. Do you want me to find out for you?'

'Yes, it would be helpful.'

'Gloria!' Pasloe called out loudly enough for his voice to echo in the office. Not for Percy's Parcels the niceties of desk-top intercom.

The door was pushed open. Nervous Gloria stood in the doorway. 'Yes, Mr Parsloe?'

'Find out when Inngey last worked for us.' Not a 'please' ... not a smile. Polite to the police, a tyrant to his staff. Hennessey and Yellich's dislike of Parsloe was both instant and great.

'Yes, Mr Parsloe.' Gloria withdrew.

Parsloe smiled at Hennessey and Yellich, who remained stone-faced. Moments later, Gloria returned and handed Parsloe a slip of paper. She withdrew without being thanked by her employer. 'He last drove for me ten days ago, and that was the last day in quite a busy period, one ... two ... nearly three weeks' work he had from us, then nothing for the last ten days. All long-distance stuff too – South Wales ... Aberdeen – would have stayed in inexpensive hotels, out one day, overnight in a bed and breakfast, back to York the next day.'

'That's interesting ... so he was out of York a lot until about ten days ago, and then he was in York?'

'Well, he wasn't away on *my* behest. Could have picked up a private load from his ad in the newsagents – they can be quite long-haul, people moving house, not enough possessions for a large removal van. I started like that, just me and a van. You can make a decent living, especially since it's all cash in hand. Suppose I shouldn't have said that.'

'Suppose you shouldn't have,' Hennessey replied icily.

'Well, long time ago. I declared enough to avoid suspicion. Anyway, now I've got a fleet of ten vans and just do parcels, no heavy lifting involved. So Inngey could still have been far and wide in the last ten days ... but not for me.'

'I see.' Hennessey shifted his position slightly. He felt very uncomfortable in his damp clothing. 'Anyway, we could find out where he had been?'

'Only if he kept a log and up-to-date accounts. If he did a journey and wanted to pocket the cash, he wouldn't have made a record of it.'

'How long has he subcontracted for you?'

'Since his own operation went under.'

'Which is how long ago?'

'About two years ago. He was a very silly man. Very silly indeed.'

'Why do you say that, Mr Parsloe?'

'Well ... he tried to muscle in on me and the other parcel-delivery companies in York. Not the way to do it. He bought a fleet of new vans, didn't even have the sense to lease them ... had them liveried with his name – "H. I. Parcel Delivery Service" – rented premises ... advertised widely ... hired drivers and waited for the phone to ring. Needless to say, the phone did not ring, his drivers sat around all day earning money for playing cards and reading newspapers, a nice holiday for a few days but after a while they got bored and wanted to work and so left him. He kept that going with his own money for nearly three months and eventually he realized he had to throw in the towel. He sold his fleet, even though they had nothing more than delivery mileage, he didn't get much for them ... they had to be re-liveried you see, sold them through the motor auctions, never a clever way to sell a motor vehicle, and barely escaped with his shirt. You build a business up like I did, and like the other parcel delivery firms did. It's your regular customers that keep you afloat, and it takes time to build up good relationships with a customer to the point that they are regular and you know how each other think. I am still surprised that Inngey didn't realize that.'

'He tried to put you out of business, and you give him work?'

'Yes,' Parsloe smiled. 'It amuses me. A fleet of new vans and now all he has is one ex-Royal Mail van, but he has a polite and a pleasant manner ... a bit toffee-nosed ... boarding-school education. Anyway, he doesn't rub up the customers the wrong way, unlike one or two of my drivers, and like I said, he's reliable and so is his machine. He really dug a massive hole for himself in doing what he did – he fell in, all the way to the bottom, and it must have cost him a lot of money. Him or someone else.' Parsloe shook his head. 'I still can't credit it, he would only have recovered half of the value of his vehicles, he paid wages to a team of men ... about ten ... and rented an industrial premises for three months, advertised massively ... and didn't make a penny. I mean, is that silly, or is that silly?'

'Hopelessly optimistic perhaps.' Hennessey was very pleased, as on previous occasions, to be a salaried man. He didn't earn a great deal of money, but it was paid into his bank account on the 16th of each month, just as a computer had been programmed to do. He didn't envy any businessman his sleepless nights and sixty-hour working week, no matter how successful he was. 'So are you going to help us to trace Mr Inngey? If you have his last address, we'd like it. Please.'

'Well, I don't know.'

'You could be prosecuted for obstructing the police,' Yellich added, allowing a menacing tone to enter his voice.

'Well ... there's no need to be offensive.'

'He's not being offensive, Mr Parsloe.' Hennessey's voice was equally stern. 'He's just advising you of the situation. We are investigating a very serious crime.'

'Oh, there's been nothing in the papers.'

'His address. If he has a motor vehicle he has to have an address.'

'Gloria!' Again Parsloe's voice echoed in his office and almost instantly, nervous Gloria opened the office door.

'Get Inngey's home address for these officers.'

'Yes, Mr Parsloe.' And the door was closed behind her. Less than a minute later she re-entered the room and again handed Parsloe a small piece of paper, clearly having copied

Inngey's address on to it from an index card. Again she withdrew without being thanked. Hennessey felt for her, Parsloe's drudge, alone in the outer office, no colleagues, no emotional warmth.

'Well, this is what I have.' Parsloe handed the paper to Hennessey. 'Not the best district of York, the Broadwood Estate.'

'Twenty-three, Simcock Avenue,' Hennessey read, 'YO94 ... not the sort of postcode to invite telephone calls from double-glazing salespeople.'

'I'll say,' Parsloe smiled. 'I live in Nether Poppleton. Came from Tang Hall ... I worked for it.'

Hennessey stood. Yellich did likewise. 'Thanks for the information. We'll see ourselves out.' The officers walked into the outer office, closing the door to Parsloe's office behind them. Gloria was typing furiously, as if working anger out of her. Hennessey walked across the office to the further door and opened it, then turned and said softly, 'You don't have to work here, you know.' Then he and Yellich exited and walked down the concrete steps to Percy's Lane. When they reached the bottom and were about to step on to the pavement, they heard the sound of high heels clicking down the stairs behind them. They turned. Gloria had put on a raincoat and hat and had grabbed her handbag.

'Thanks,' she said when she joined Hennessey and Yellich at the street door. 'I just wanted someone to say that to me.'

Hennessey and Yellich walked back to Micklegate Bar Police Station through easing rain, a wintry sun becoming increasingly visible through widening breaks in the cloud layer. Having signed in, they sat in Hennessey's office, drinking tea from china mugs.

'Has the luck of the devil,' Hennessey said. 'By all accounts.'

'Doesn't he ... by all accounts.' Yellich found the tea refreshing. It was just what he – and, he suspected, Hennessey too – needed. It had been a wet afternoon and there was work still to be done. 'Floors a security bloke, then gets a job with the company his victim worked for, tries to put parcel delivery companies out of business, then makes a living subcontracting for one of them. I have met people like that before ... they have a knack of bouncing back and landing on their feet.'

'There's a story to that treasure chest. Any news from the auctioneers yet?'

'None. I'll nudge them, if you like.'

'Do that on Monday if we don't hear tomorrow.'

'Very good, boss.'

'Any ideas?' Hennessey sipped his tea.

'About?'

'The murders ... the motive ... the culprit.'

'Yes ... rather keep them to myself ... too early in the piece to jump ahead.'

'Probably.'

'But I am growing anxious to meet Harold Inngey.'

'So am I,' Hennessey smiled. He glanced at the clock on the wall of this office: 16.02 hours. 'No time like the present.'

With Yellich as usual at the wheel, the officers drove out to the Broadwood Estate, to Simcock Avenue. As Yellich turned into the avenue, they noticed a red van parked against the kerb halfway along. Clearly ex-Royal Mail, with a vertically sliding rear door.

'No need to look for twenty-three,' Yellich said, driving towards the van and subsequently parking behind it.

The house had a blue-painted door and a garden which seemed to be managed, chopped back, rather than caringly tended. They went to the front door and Yellich knocked on it with the classic police officer's knock ... tap, tap ... tap. They heard movement from within the house. Then a voice called out, 'Go round the back.' The voice had a Yorkshire accent. Hennessey and Yellich walked down the side of the red-brick council house, past dustbins hidden by a wooden screen, round the corner to the back of the house, where a small lawn was bounded by high privet. The roofs of the houses in the next street could be seen above the privet. It was by then 4.30 p.m. and many houses had lights burning. Hennessey tapped on the back door. It was opened quickly. The man who stood in the doorway was tall, muscular, clean-shaven. Hennessey thought that women would find him attractive.

'Yes?' He had a manner which seemed to the officers to be defensive, a slight hostility mixed with the curious.

'Mr Inngey?'

'Yes.'

'Police.'

'Yes?'

'May we come in? We have a few questions we'd like to ask you ... and some information.'

'My family?'

'Yes ... how did you know?'

'You'd better come in.'

Hennessey and Yellich stepped straight into the living room of the house, clearly no porch or scullery in these houses. The living room itself was small and had a cramped feel when three men, two police officers and an ex-Royal Marine, stood in it. A fire burned in the grate, small, struggling for life. Coke mainly, but a lump of coal had been placed on it, illegal in a smokeless zone, but coal has a homely quality that coke does not possess, and Hennessey could understand the appeal it held. He certainly wouldn't be making an issue of it.

'Please take a seat.' Inngey had lost his Yorkshire accent and spoke with what Hennessey believed to be called 'Received Pronunciation', not dissimilar to the perfect enunciation of a newsreader. Hennessey and Inngey sat in armchairs at either side of the fire. Yellich sat in an upright chair next to a narrow table by the window. A pool of water had gathered on the windowsill, clearly from that afternoon's rainfall.

'So, my family?' Inngey said, and having noted Hennessey's surprise at his change of accent he said, 'Survival technique. I learned it in the Marines. Doesn't do to be too posh unless you're an officer, and then it's expected. Learned the same in prison. And it's come in useful here on the estate. I'd get my windows put in if I put on the dog here.'

'I see. How do you know we want to talk to you about your family, Mr Inngey?'

'By family, I mean parents and brother and sister. Not wife or children.'

'Yes ... we mean that too, the residents of the Manor House at Long Hundred.'

'Yes. What of them?'

'Well, I am afraid we have some bad news for you, Mr Inngey...'

'Oh...' Inngey sat back in his chair, releasing a flow of warmth from the fire which reached Yellich. 'They're dead.'

'I'm afraid so. If it is your parents and younger siblings ... they still have to be identified. That will have to be done by DNA matching.'

'Not by sight, as you see on television?'

'Not on this occasion. They were found a

few days ago, and in suspicious circumstances. There had to be a post-mortem. I
am sorry we couldn't find you earlier, but
you are a difficult person to locate.'

'Yes ... I have cut myself off from them, in
terms of distance.'

'It doesn't seem to surprise you that they
are deceased. Nor do you seem particularly
bothered.'

'Well, we do keep in touch. I live apart
from them but we have always known where
each other is. They would phone me whenever they left the house ... from a call box ...
they don't have a phone in the house.'

'Yes, we have been in the house ... well,
very interesting.'

'What happened?'

'We were hoping you might be able to tell
us, Mr Inngey.'

Inngey paused. His face hardened. 'Suspicious circumstances ... are you saying that I
am under suspicion?'

'Well, yes, in the sense that everybody connected with the family is under suspicion.'

'There is nobody else connected with the
family!'

Hennessey raised an eyebrow.

'Oh, that was very clever,' Inngey snarled

at Hennessey. 'Enjoy trapping people, do you?'

'Well, you could say I get paid for it. Among other things.'

'What else do you get paid for?'

'Protecting the public.' Hennessey allowed a cold edge to enter his voice. 'You went to the house last week.'

'Did I?'

'So we are informed.'

'Who by?'

'Can't tell you.'

'No comment then, can't reply to that statement, it's hearsay.'

'All right. When did you last visit the Manor House at Long Hundred?'

'Last week.' Inngey shrugged. 'I won't deny it, especially since I was seen. Arthur Styles, I bet. His farmland borders our house. You can throw a stone from our front door into his wheat field ... or oilseed ... whatever he grows now, probably the latter. All that lovely EEC subsidy for growing brilliant yellow plants instead of wheat. He keeps an eye on the house. Not a protective eye, more of a resentful eye. If it wasn't for my parents, the Styleses would be the top family in Long Hundred. We don't have any

154

money, we don't employ anybody, but the Manor House and the woodland that goes with the manor give my parents a certain social clout that the Styleses don't have. So Styles just keeps his covetous eye on the house. It would be just like him to have noticed me.'

'So when did you visit?'

'Well ... Thursday today ... probably early last week, Tuesday, perhaps Wednesday.'

'Why?'

'Why what?'

'Why did you visit? You are estranged from them ... partially so, anyway. So why did you visit?'

'I hadn't heard from them for a few days. I went to see if all was well.'

'And was it?'

'They were not at home. I assumed they were out. So I came back here.'

'That was over a week ago. You didn't return? I mean if you were curious ... . Did you check whether their car was there?'

'No ... it never occurred to me.'

'It didn't occur to you! Your parents and younger siblings allegedly went everywhere together, even if only going to the shops ... and always in their old Jaguar. The house was empty and you didn't check to see if the car wasn't in the outbuildings where they kept it? Seems strange. I would have thought that it was the logical thing to do.'

'Well, I just didn't ... that's it. I thought, Oh they're out, and came back here. So where were they found? What happened to them?'

'You don't know?' Hennessey saw Yellich stiffen. Both officers knew an arrest was probably imminent. At the very least, a request to accompany the officers to the police station for formal interview under the Police and Criminal Evidence Act.

'No. I don't know. Tell me. Please.'

'They were found in Edgefield House.'

'Edgefield!'

'Yes, I understand that the old house has some significance for your family?'

'It's our ancestral home ... we are gentry ... it's hard to believe, but I am now the seventh Lord Inngey. And my home is a council house, about one mile from our ancestral home.'

'Tell us about the treasure?'

Inngey shot a glance at Hennessey. 'Who have you been talking to?'

Hennessey paused; the coal crackled,

flared, then died again to a warm glow. 'I'd rather not tell you.'

'That means you won't.'

'If you like.'

'I think I can probably guess. Little Miss Hewlett?'

'Perhaps. Perhaps not. The treasure...?'

'Well, there is rumoured to be a chest containing valuables which is handed down to each firstborn son upon the death of his father.'

'Rumoured?'

'Yes ... just a rumour.'

'I see ... you haven't searched for it?'

'No. I don't believe it exists. If it does, it can't be worth much, just a pile of junk really. Do you think my parents would be living in that old, damp house if they had any money?' Inngey smiled. 'I mean, really ... hidden treasure ... it's the stuff of fiction, children's fiction at that.'

'You didn't search for it?'

'I just told you, no.'

'Either at Edgefield House or the Manor House?'

'Do you have difficulty understanding plain, simple English? No. No. No. I haven't searched for it. I doubt it exists.'

157

'All right, we'll come back to that.'

'What do you mean, you'll come back to that? There is no chest of goodies.'

'Well somebody broke into the Manor House and searched for something.'

'Did they?' Inngey sounded genuine. There was concern in his voice.

'Yes, someone did. Forced the front door. Searched the attic.'

'I see.'

'Do you have keys for the Manor House, Mr Inngey?'

'No.'

'But it's your family home.'

'No.' Inngey's jaw set firm. 'This is my family home. This little council box. And I am my family.'

'You left home early?'

'Yes ... nothing wrong in that.'

'Joined the armed services?'

'Royal Marines, as I said. I was in for nearly ten years. I survived despite being taken for a snob by the NCOs ... one corporal in particular ... he had me up on a charge for sewing a button on my tunic with "the wrong colour black" – I ask you ... I could cope because I could rise above the mentality, and stayed in, gradually won over

158

the NCOs.'

'You didn't want a commission ... a man with your background?'

'I was escaping.'

'Escaping?'

'Home. I do not consider myself to be psychiatrically ill.'

'I don't think you are, either.'

'I am the only one that isn't.'

'The only one?'

'Of my family. There was just something wrong with them. My parents and younger brother and sister ... even when we were kids ... there was the sense that they were four of a kind and that I was on the outside. They were not dangerously ill ... just ... well ... "dotty". It's difficult to explain ... they just seemed to think in the same way, and how they thought was just alien to me. They'd sit in a group, all talking at once ... outstanding ... they'd communicate with each other ... all talking at the same time ... then they'd stop talking in an instant as though powered from the same source and somebody had pulled the plug ... then after a pause, they'd all start talking again at the same moment. I mean the stopping of the conversation, the pause, the restart, was as if they all shared the same personality but it was sufficiently different for them to talk to each other ... but they never argued ... they always agreed with each other. Then there was me in the household ... pushed to the edge ... it was like that from about the time my brother and sister were about seven or eight and I was in my late teens.'

'Quite an age gap.'

'Yes, there is, and things changed when they grew old enough to become personalities. I began to get edged out at about the time that I was old enough to leave home anyway ... too lazy and ill-disciplined to go to university, didn't have the bits of paper anyway, so it was the armed services ... and the Marines, 'cos they have a nicer dress uniform. I tell you, in the Regiment I found security. It was very refreshing.'

'When did you hear about the treasure chest?'

'Will you leave that alone! There is no such chest ... it's a fantasy.'

'Just answer the question.'

'All right. When I was about fourteen or fifteen, one of the rare conversations I had with my father, he told me about the chest when he told me of the family history. The family lost its fortune in a tin-mine deal ... in Bolivia.'

'Tin? Bolivia?'

'Yes ... Tin ... Bolivia.'

'Not silver in Argentina?'

'Ah...' Inngey smiled. 'So you have been talking to little Miss Hewlett. It was tin in Bolivia. I told her silver in Argentina. I don't know why ... perhaps it sounded a little more romantic. Silver in the pampas ... Bolivia isn't really a country associated with romance. But it was a harmless lie ... tin or silver, Argentina or Bolivia. What do the details matter? The gist is that one of my ancestors was greedy and stupid. He handed over the family fortune in exchange for a half-share in a mine which didn't exist. That scam is as old as the hills ... I dare say it still goes on. I dare say you will find somebody who will buy the Humber Bridge or Leeds and Bradford Airport if somebody offers it for sale.'

'All right. So yes, we talked to Ms Hewlett. So tell us why you lied to us?'

Inngey's face hardened. 'I have not lied to you.'

'You haven't?'

'No.'

'You and Miss Hewlett did not search Edgefield House from cellar to rafter, looking for the treasure chest?'

Inngey paled. 'No. No. No. Edgefield House is a shell. There is nothing inside it. Heavens, ponder the stupidity of leaving a chest of valuables in an old deserted house, where it could be found by anybody or go up in smoke at any time.'

'Well, stranger things have happened, but yes ... it does beggar belief. But you do have money problems, you have the motivation to search for a box of treasure.'

'Who hasn't got money problems?'

'But you have acute money problems. Your business collapsed.'

'I paid all my creditors.'

'With somebody else's money.'

'So Hewlett has a score to settle, but she went in with her eyes open ... and she still has her house ... she'll just have to work to pay off the mortgage, like everybody else.'

'Did you like your family?'

'What sort of question is that?'

'It is a police officer's question in a murder investigation ... a multiple-murder investigation ... so just answer it.'

Inngey paused. 'No, I didn't.'

'Did you like them at all?'

'No. If you must know ... not at all. I was driven out. I had no positive feelings for either of my parents or my siblings ... Like I said, they were as mad as a bunch of March hares, the four of them, and I was happily outside that little circle ... the safety in the Regiment, two tours of Northern Ireland, but in a safe period, no major conflicts ... but ... I tell you, from my experience I think the person that invented families ought to be shot.'

'Who else did you tell about the mythical treasure chest?'

'Well ... Hewlett, of course ... the blokes in the Regiment but only to say it was a family myth, something to laugh about over our Tiger Beer when we were in Singapore ... or whatever we drank at any particular posting ... Guinness in Northern Ireland. We always used to have a favourite drink in each posting.'

'Anybody else might know of the treasure?'

'Which doesn't exist? I have no way of knowing.'

'Might your parents have mentioned it?'

'They might ... as might my brother and

sister ... but you really have no way of asking them, have you? Why are you so obsessed with the treasure anyway?'

'Because we found it.'

Inngey's jaw dropped.

'It's being valued as we speak. I think you've been less than truthful, Mr Inngey.'

'You've found it!' Inngey's face paled. Hennessey thought it was a good act, so good it might not be an act. 'What's in it? Where is it?'

'At the premises of an auction house. And where was it? It was where you thought it would be. In the attic of Edgefield House. As you believed.'

'I believed...?' Inngey seemed to struggle for words. 'I believe ... look, I have told you what I thought about the likelihood of the treasure existing and the likelihood that it would be in the ruin.'

'But you and Ms Hewlett looked for it.'

'We did not!'

'We have information that you did.'

'From whom?'

'We can't tell you.' Hennessey paused. 'You have a criminal record, Mr Inngey.'

Inngey shrugged. 'No point in denying it.'

'For violence and theft.'

'Theft?'

'Embezzlement.'

'I took what was mine. I earned it. I opened the safe, there were thousands in there, I took the one and a half thousand that was mine.'

'Your actual property?'

'Commission that was owed to me. The guy said I hadn't earned it, pointed to some sub-clause hidden in my contract. It was technically embezzlement, but he was stealing from me.'

'But you have stolen. In the eyes of the law, you are a thief.'

'Are? Perhaps was ... I consider myself an honest man. I scratch a living carrying stuff in the back of my van ... be the easiest thing in the world to stop on the journey, help myself to anything I might fancy, but I don't. I never have and I never will ... other men with vans can't say that, not all, anyway.'

'You learned to kill people in the Marines?'

'Yes.'

'By breaking necks?'

'Among other ways.'

'You dislike your family, you need money

... being a man with a van is too tame for you ... you searched for the treasure. You're ruthless enough to use the equity in Samantha Hewlett's home to finance a parcel delivery company which you expected to be an instant success. You're arrogant enough to steal money you believe belongs to you, despite what the letter of the law might say ... and you have the ability to snap necks ... which is how your family was killed.'

'Their necks were broken?'

'After they had been deprived of food for a few days ... perhaps to encourage them to divulge the whereabouts of the treasure chest.'

'This is ridiculous, no man would do that to his family.'

'Mr Inngey, I have been a police officer nearly all my long working life and I can assure you that you would be startled by what people have done to their families ... and murdering for financial gain ... even amongst the next of kin, is nothing new.'

'I want a lawyer.'

Hennessey smiled. 'We'll provide one for you. Do you have a coat? It's getting cold outside.'

'Where are we going?'

'To the police station.' Hennessey stood. Yellich stood as well. 'Harold Inngey, I am arresting you in connection with the murders of Lord Inngey and Lady Inngey and their children, Anne and Percy. It may harm your defence if you do not mention, when questioned, anything you may rely on in court.' He paused. 'Where do you keep your coat?'

George Hennessey was on his way home. He went over the interview in his mind as he drove out to Easingwold. He, Yellich, Inngey and the duty solicitor, Esther Pinder: young, slender, humourless, but with a brain as sharp as a tack, and more threatening, fighting more aggressively because she and Inngey had seemed to 'click' without crossing the boundary which separated them as lawyer and client; they clearly liked each other. She had systematically unpicked Hennessey's argument: it was wholly circumstantial, and some points were not even that, just mere speculation. There was no need for Lord Inngey – she had insisted on using his title throughout, as if she thrilled to it – no need for Lord Inngey to break into the Manor House because, if he had abducted the late Lord Inngey, he would have access to his house keys, and the house keys of Lady Inngey and of Percy Inngey and of Anne Inngey, a point which Hennessey had to concede.

Miss Pinder delivered a devastating attack on the motive. It was incomprehensible that a man should attempt to torture anyone to reveal the whereabouts of a treasure hoard which neither person believed to exist. Until the chest had been discovered by the police, the existence of the hoard had been believed to be a myth. The allegation by Miss Hewlett, that she and Inngey had searched Edgefield House, was unsubstantiated. Miss Pinder had insisted that Lord Inngey be either charged or released from custody.

As Inngey and Miss Pinder were leaving the station, Hennessey heard Inngey ask, with the polished charm of the English peerage, whether Miss Pinder had eaten that day.

'I haven't, actually,' she had said. 'An early dinner sounds a very good idea ... but if you take me to dinner, you can't engage my professional services.'

'I am sure you can recommend another good solicitor.' He smiled and held out his arm. She took it and they left the police station walking closely side by side.

Hennessey had turned away. He realized that even in the early twenty-first century, inherited titles still mean something, especially if the holder of the title is also in possession of a chest of very valuable valuables. That can make even a council-house-dwelling, self-employed van driver an attractive proposition for a youthful, husband-hunting lawyer.

Hennessey arrived at his home in Easingwold, a four-bedroom detached house on Thirsk Road. He let himself in the front door and was greeted by a barking, tail-wagging Oscar. He and the small brown mongrel went out on to the patio at the rear of the house, Oscar exiting through the ever open dog flap in the back door, and while Oscar criss-crossed the lawn, with his tail still wagging in delight at Hennessey's return, Hennessey told the garden of his day, or so an observer would have thought. But George Hennessey, he of silver hair and liver-spotted hands, was not talking to the garden, nor to himself, but to his lovely, lovely wife, taken from him, cruelly young, aged just twenty-four years and a few months after the birth of their son. Jennifer's ashes had been scattered on the garden; and upon coming home each day, George Hennessey would stand in the back garden, no matter what the weather, and tell Jennifer of his day. Recently that summer, he had also told her of another, new woman in his life, that they were right for each other, that he hoped she wouldn't mind, that she understood his love for her was not at all diminished, and after he had spoken, he experienced a glow, a warmth, which could not alone be explained by the warmth of the rays of the late-afternoon sun.

That day, as if bidden by some unseen and unrecognized influence, his thoughts turned to the way Jennifer and he had met: the way their eyes had met across the room at the wedding reception, he being a friend of the groom, she a relative of the bride ... both, they found, had come from the south of England and had settled in Yorkshire – he from London; she from Hertfordshire ... it was the first of many, many things they were to discover that they had in common. During that reception they had moved gradually further and further away from the main body of guests until they sat together on a bench outside the hotel enjoying the summer afternoon and talking as if they had known each other for many, many years ... utterly relaxed and at peace in one another's company. After that meeting their affair and subsequent marriage had been inevitable ... the holiday in Portugal ... making love on a bed of bluebells in an English woodland, afterwards lying naked under the canopy of trees listening to the birdsong, laughing softly, agreeing that 'doing it' had proved harder than they both had thought it would be ... the bluebells had seemed such an inviting bed ... Their honeymoon ... a cycling holiday in Ireland ... the day they moved into their house ... Jennifer taking a glance at the back garden and saying, 'We can do better than that...' The day she told him that she was pregnant. That evening, memories and more memories flooded into his mind ... She was, he believed, responding to him for being there ... for not forgetting her ... for telling her of his day. It was another sort of glow ... another sort of warmth.

He returned indoors and prepared a wholesome casserole, just the thing, he reasoned, to keep out the chill of the November evenings. After he had eaten, he settled down to read a recent addition to his collection of books about military history. It was an obscure, but well-written account of trench warfare in the Great War, told in a simple and clear style and of such honesty that it made reference to junior officers masturbating to ease the stress – a brave admission, and a brave publisher who published it amid the prudery and primness of the 1920s. Finishing the account, on a whim, when feeling a sudden curiosity, he stood and took his best dictionary from the shelf and consulted it ... one word led to another ... 'Well' ... This time he did speak to himself. 'Well,' he said, 'well I never. How interesting.' He then gave Oscar his supper, after which, man and dog, loving each other's company, went for their evening walk. Upon returning, Hennessey, leaving Oscar in the house, walked into Easingwold for a pint of mild, just one, before last orders were called.

Five

... in which a return visit to Long Hundred is made and with it, a disturbing discovery. Later, the gentle reader meets DS Yellich's home circumstances.

FRIDAY, 12.00 HOURS – 22.00 HOURS

Hennessey and Yellich drove out of York to Long Hundred. As they turned off the main road and into the village, Yellich remarked on the strangeness of its name.

'I looked it up last night.' Hennessey glanced around him. 'It occurred to me that we had better take the measure of the village, the key to solving this murder lies in this village, I am convinced of it. So I looked up "Hundred" in my old dictionary, to see if it had another meaning beside the product of ten multiplied by ten.'

'And it does?'

'It's an ancient Saxon term for a division of land, containing one hundred hides.'

'Hides, skipper?' Yellich halted the car outside the Three Horsehoes. 'Like animal hides?'

Hennessey gave Yellich a pained look. 'In fairness, I didn't know what a hide was in that sense, so I looked that up as well. It's another ancient division of land which was deemed to be of sufficient size for one family to be able to subsist if they worked it.'

'I see ... keeping pigs and growing crops.'

'I would imagine.' Hennessey looked about him. The village appeared deserted. It was a cold, dry autumn day although the sky was blue and a photograph taken of the village that day would look akin to a summer's day. 'So one hundred hides and you have a single hundred ... it's a bit like calling it "Long Acre" or "Long Square Mile".'

'Well, you live and learn.' Yellich opened the driver's door, as Hennessey opened his door, the passenger door. Hennessey had a great dislike of motor vehicles for a deeply personal reason and drove only if necessary. In the city, he walked if at all possible; when driving out of the city, he was content to let someone else drive.

They got out of the car and each man drew a sharp intake of breath between clenched teeth as the cold hit their bodies. Hennessey smiled at Yellich. 'Let's get inside.'

The interior of the Three Horseshoes Hennessey found pleasingly solid, a lot of darkly stained wood, horse-brasses hanging on the wall, beams in the ceiling and a carpet of red upon which was a busy pattern in dark blue and grey. There was only one patron, an elderly lady, who sat in front of a schooner of sherry. She wore a yellow bonnet and a grey coat and mumbled to herself. The publican did indeed look very dissimilar to Arthur Styles. It was easy to see why folk did not believe they were brothers, despite what might be written on their birth certificates. He was taller than Arthur Styles, significantly so, slender, had a warmth about him which might be superficial and liable to change at the slightest provocation. Further, Hennessey, upon first meeting the man, just could not envisage him creeping up on people as his brother was wont to do. 'Yes, gents, what can I get you?' He spoke with a soft, yet distinct York-shire accent, more homely than hard and aggressive.

'Police.' Hennessey flashed his ID. Yellich did likewise.

'No trouble, I hope?'

'No, sir.' Hennessey spoke reassuringly. 'We'd like to ask you a few questions, per-haps you could help us. We have come to you because the pub seems a good place to start.'

'Start what?' The publican's smile revealed gold-capped teeth. He had a wedding ring and wore a gold bracelet on his right wrist. A watch with a heavy leather strap wound round his left wrist.

'Asking questions about the village.'

'About the village? About us, little us? Is it in connection with the murder at the Manor House?'

'About the murder of the people who lived in the Manor House, yes.'

'That's right ... said on the news last night, couldn't tell where they were murdered, but it was the Inngey family ... all four ... the other brother lived away from home. So how can I help you?'

'By telling us what you know about the

family, or pointing us in the direction of anyone who can. We know they kept themselves to themselves and went everywhere together.'

'Yes, they were strange ... came in here once or twice but not very often and never when it was crowded. Didn't want to mix with the riff-raff ... hadn't any money, poor as church mice, but that blue blood ... well, they kept themselves apart, aloof as well.'

'What was the feeling in the village about them?'

'Well...' The publican, Arnold Styles by the plaque screwed to the wall behind the bar, shrugged. 'What can I say? Not popular, but not unpopular, they were ... tolerated. They had the Manor House ... that made them the top family in Long Hundred, but they made little contribution to the village.'

'Top family'. The expression clanged in Hennessey's mind. He was unused to rural policing, but despite that had never come across a village which was so self-conscious about putting families in a caste-system-like hierarchy.

'Only ever came to the pub once in a blue moon, and never spent much. I think that was the reason why they were not liked, but like I said, not disliked either.'

'Tolerated, as you said.'

'Aye, as I said. You see, this is a settled village, I mean settled in its ways. I grew up here. My family have farmed here for generations. I opted for the softer life of a publican.' He slapped the solid wooden bar with a resounding slap which caused the lady in the yellow bonnet to stop her mumblings and cry out in alarm. 'All right, Mary,' Arnold Styles called to her, 'just me talking to these two gentlemen from the city ... called in to see little us.' He smiled at Hennessey and Yellich. 'Mary's about my most regular regular ... a widow ... lost her husband on the land.'

'On the land?'

'Farming accident. It tends to make rural folk angry when all that fuss is made about accidents in coal mines, or when they hear about labourers getting "danger money" in steelworks, because farming is the most dangerous occupation in Britain.'

'Is it?'

'Yes, it is ... more than fifty deaths per year ... averages out at more than one a week ... accidents with machinery, getting gored by bulls or crushed by cows or horses ... often made worse because sometimes there is no one else around to give first aid, or rescue someone or raise the alarm, so a body is found in circumstances where if it had happened in the city, there'd be folk milling round and dialling for an ambulance on their mobile phones.'

'I can see that,' Hennessey said. 'Didn't know it was the most dangerous occupation.'

'Statistically it is. An awful lot more farm-hands are killed each year in the course of their work than police officers. Anyway, Mary lost her husband on the land, her pension doesn't go far but she's always outside when I open for the day at eleven a.m. and she has two large sherries ... mutters and mumbles away to herself, spinning out her drinks as long as she can, and leaves about one to one thirty p.m. every day. If she doesn't turn up, it will mean she's unwell, and I'll ask someone to check up on her. But the Inngeys ... well, you see, if you are a top family in this village, you are expected to find work for the bottom families, but they didn't put any money into the village ... never bought anything from the shops, went to the supermarket in Malton in their old car rather than buy in the grocery store. I mean, if they ran out of milk or teabags then, yes, they'd buy locally, but in the main it was twice or three times a week to the supermarket in Malton. Anything else they bought in the village would be stamps from the post office and such like.'

'Anybody that you know have a particular grudge against them?'

'Ah ... now ... come to think of it, you might have struck a very useful nail on the head there.'

'Oh?'

'You could talk to Nancy Braithwaite.'

'Who is she? And why?'

'Well, Nancy ... not seen her for a day or two, not that unusual, not as unusual as if I hadn't seen Old Mary there for a day or two, but she's from a bottom family in Long Hundred and she "did" for the Inngeys. I suppose, in fairness, I should say they got that right, didn't spend hardly anything in the village, but they did employ Nancy to come and clean for them three times a week. She was with them for about ten years ... never missed a shift ... and kept her family going on what the Inngeys paid her,

her family being her old dad ... he died a few months ago ... but Nancy got the sack ... "You need not come again"...'

'Just like that?'

'Yep.' Arnold Styles grimaced and raised his eyebrows. 'Just like that ... no reason given, not in so many words, but the suggestion of theft was in the air and that more than anything annoyed Nancy. She was cut up about that, then the anger turned to resentment. She had a key to let herself in when they were not at home, and all the time she was cleaning for them, not a penny nor a farthing was lost from the house, and then there was the suggestion that something had gone missing and, without making a clear accusation, they took the door key off her and told her not to come back. So I was told. Didn't get that from Nancy herself, the story went round that that was what happened.'

'Interesting. When was that?'

'Summertime ... yes ... I remember the light nights. I saw her one evening ... late ... after last orders. I take my animal for a walk, he gets his main walk before we open for the day, but after that he's shut in the yard and the house ... there's a dog flap.'

181

'Yes,' Hennessey smiled. 'I have the same arrangement in my house.'

'Really? What have you got?'

'Small mongrel dog.'

'Alsatian. I need a big dog to protect the premises, but a big dog needs exercise. We go out for an hour in the morning, but then he's cooped up all day, so he needs to get out in the evening, so I take him for a run on the green. He takes himself for a walk really, running backwards and forwards for half an hour, burning off all that pent-up energy, but it was one such evening when Rascal was pounding backwards and forwards from one end of the green to the other, I heard the sound of a heavy footfall ... clomp, clomp, clomp. I turned and saw Nancy Braithwaite walking towards her cottage, a really angry woman, stamping her heels into the road surface ... totally obsessed ... walked right past me, don't even think she saw me. Never seen her like that, normally she was a light-stepping woman but she was not a happy woman that night, not best pleased at all. Though she was able to support her father in the last days of his life. So she has an axe to grind against Their Lord and Ladyship ... they were titled, did you know that?'

'Yes,' Hennessey nodded. 'Yes, we knew that. Hereditary, they didn't do anything to earn it ... doesn't carry any political weight any more.'

'Aye ... thank goodness.'

'So, where can we find Nancy Braithwaite?'

'Dunno...' Styles smiled, 'give in. Where can you find her? But I can tell you where her cottage is.'

'That'll be useful.' Hennessey returned the smile, sharing the joke.

'Well ... right out of the door, keep to the right of the green, just follow the line of cottages, last road off on the right is an unadopted road ... poor surface, full of potholes ... they'll be full of water this time of year ... the road is called Scrivener's Folly and Nancy's cottage is the last cottage on the right before the fields begin.'

'Thanks.'

'Watch her dog.'

'Big?'

'Collie ... but very aggressive ... but she keeps it well under control.'

The two officers left the Three Horsehoses and turned right, as directed, wrapping their coats about them against the keen wind, whose chill factor Hennessey guessed was pushing the air temperature down to freezing. And it was still only November. It was going to be a hard winter, he thought, and said so in order to break the silence between him and Yellich.

'Aye,' Yellich replied. 'Mind you, that's probably no bad thing, the recent winters have all been mild ... lot of sickly growth about ... needs a prolonged period of freezing to kill it off and allow new growth. We just need to be sure we have our winter warmers on, take the mothballs out of the long johns.'

They walked on in further silence until they came to Scrivener's Folly and found it to be as the merry publican had warned: unadopted, a muddy, gravelly surface, deeply rutted and potholed and by then, full of brown rainwater.

'Very unadopted, I'd say.' Yellich glanced at the potholes. Many were wide, craters more than potholes, and all looked deep. Scrivener's Folly drove a narrow gap between half-timbered cottages, each of which stood in a modest garden, out towards the fields, then brown and rich and tilled, bounded by naked hedgerows, towards a black wood, and all under a high blue sky. A photograph of that scene, unlike a photograph of the village, would say 'autumn' or 'winter' despite the colour of the sky. A lace curtain flicked open and then shut in the window of the cottage nearest to the officers. Both Hennessey and Yellich saw the curtain twitch.

'We are not alone on this island, boss.'

Hennessey chuckled. 'Aye, I have heard that about the country ... you are being watched, wherever you go ... don't see anybody but they see you and strangers are identified in an instant. Give me the anonymity of the city any time. Well, let's go and visit Miss Braithwaite.'

Hennessey and Yellich picked their way along Scrivener's Folly. They started out together, side by side, but by keeping their eyes on their feet and focusing on their own progress had, by the time they had gone no more than ten paces, been separated from one another, with Hennessey finding easy going and relatively high ground on the left of the road. Yellich struggled on the right-hand side of the road, where there seemed to be more water than road and found himself forced to leap in places in order to maintain forward progress, much to Hennessey's amusement.

'Wet side and dry side,' Hennessey remarked.

'Aye...' Yellich growled, positioning himself to leap across a pothole, 'and where did my Donald Duck take me?'

Eventually, by means slow and careful, Hennessey and Yellich reached the gate of the last cottage on the right-hand side. They stood looking at it. It was squat, half-timbered, like the other cottages in Long Hundred, but unlike the majority of cottages, it had a neglected look. The garden was overgrown, the paint was faded and had peeled away in places, the roof tiles seemed a loose and disjointed mess. The curtains were closed.

'Looks deserted,' Hennessey said.

'Does, doesn't it? The publican didn't say this lady worked now, did he? He didn't indicate that she had found alternative employment after getting the chop from the Inngeys.'

'No, he didn't. It's quiet too – no noise, no radio, no daytime TV.' Hennessey paused. 'You know, Yellich, I am an old copper, I have an old copper's waters, my instincts are honed as much as they will be.'

'I know what you are going to say, skipper.' Yellich too looked at the quiet cottage, squat, with a stillness about it that seemed sinister.

'What am I going to say?'

'That you've got a bad feeling about this building. I may not have your old waters, but I have a bad feeling too. A very uncomfortable feeling.'

'So we are of like mind. We proceed with caution.'

Hennessey opened the gate. It creaked loudly enough to be heard inside the cottage, yet no dog barked. Their shoes sounded on the concrete path as they approached the house ... still no bark ... only when Hennessey knocked on the door did they elicit a response from the interior of the cottage, and that was in the form of a meek and feeble whine from within. Hennessey and Yellich glanced at each other and then both unhesitatingly put their shoulders to the door. The interior of the cottage was spartan, smelled of damp. The collie limped towards them with its tongue swollen and protruding, tail between its legs. Hennessey turned to the sink unit, poured a bowl of water from which the collie drank deeply. They moved out of the kitchen and into the living room. In the gloom of the room both officers could make out the form of a woman, tied to an upright chair.

'Dead,' Hennessey said.

'Oh, very, I would say, skipper.'

'We need SOCO ... police surgeon ... a sergeant and four constables.'

'Very good, boss.' Yellich reached for his mobile.

'And the RSPCA ... get them to send someone along a.s.a.p. to collect the dog. The thing hasn't been fed and watered for days ... the body must be about four or five days old. Can you find a leash, take the dog back to our car, tell the animal cruelty folk to take it from the car when they come ... . ask the publican to keep an eye on it.'

'Shall I feed it?'

'No,' Hennessey shook his head. 'It will survive for another hour, we mustn't disturb the crime scene. But we want the animal well away.'

'Sorry, boss, I wasn't thinking.' Yellich searched for the lead and slipped it on the collie, which was drinking deeply from the generous bowl of water Hennessey had placed on the floor. He stepped outside out of habit, formed when he radioed for assistance, and switched on his mobile phone. He phoned Micklegate Bar Police Station, just the one phone call, giving his location and asking for a Scenes of Crime Officer, the police surgeon and uniformed assistance. He also asked for the RSPCA to be contacted and provided details of where they could collect Nancy Braithwaite's allegedly aggressive, but by then weakened and traumatized, dog. He returned inside the house, took the dog gently by the lead and eased it away from the bowl.

'Ask the publican to give it more water,' Hennessey said, 'and don't let it drink from puddles.'

'Very good, boss.'

Hennessey waited for Yellich to clear the bungalow, then he too stepped outside. He closed the door behind him. He looked about him. An adjacent cottage, a cottage opposite. He stepped over the low wooden fence which divided Nancy Braithwaite's cottage from her adjacent neighbour's cottage and knocked on the door. It would be some time before SOCO and the police surgeon arrived, and so, Hennessey reasoned, he should use the time to commence house-to-house inquiries. The door of the neighbour's cottage was opened swiftly upon his knocking, swiftly both in terms of the time which elapsed between his knock and the bolt being drawn across on the inside, and swiftly in terms of the speed with which the door was opened. The occupant was a small-boned woman with a sharp face, who seemed to Hennessey to be much driven by curiosity. She looked to be about twenty-five.

'Aye?' She had a sharp, aggressive way of talking, the smell of a meal being prepared emanated from behind her and did not whet Hennessey's appetite, smelling, he thought, like turnips being boiled.

'Police.' Hennessey showed his ID.

'Thought you were ... saw you going into Nancy's house.'

'You saw us break in?'

'Aye ... but knew you were police ... middle of the day ... both were putting the door in, not one with the other one keeping an eye out. Only the police would do that.'

'Reasonable deduction.' Hennessey pursed his lips. 'And yes, it is about Ms Braith-waite.'

'Miss,' the young woman replied smugly. 'She never wed, did Nancy, never.' From behind her, an infant began to cry. The woman glanced behind her with a look of hostility that caused Hennessey to fear for the day-to-day welfare of her child. She turned back to Hennessey. 'She'll go to sleep soon.'

'Did you see much of Miss Braithwaite?'

'Well, you see how close we live, we both of us keep house ... only she keeps for her-self ... I keep for my man and me and her.' She spoke with pride. Hennessey thought her to be about five feet tall.

'When did you last see her?'

'Nancy? A few days ago. Didn't see her every day.'

'So you were not concerned when you didn't see her for a few days?'

'Nope. I have a house to keep and she lives quietly ... well, she does ... her dog's a prize terror. I saw your mate taking him away. Going to put him down, are you?'

'I hope not, and "we" won't be doing any-thing to it or with it.'

'Well, you know what I meant.' She sniffed

indignantly. She was not a woman who liked to be corrected. He imagined her husband to be a large, affable, easily-led man. He had heard, and indeed observed, that there is a chemistry, quite mysterious to observers, which makes the union between small, sharp-tempered women, and large, gentle men, work.

'When did you last see Miss Braithwaite?'

'Nancy ... well, Friday now ... must be the beginning of the week ... no ... longer ... must have been the weekend ... yes, Sunday ... time flies, eh? Yes it was Sunday, my man remarked that she wouldn't do that with such effort if she had to do it all week like I had to.'

'Do what?'

'Labour.'

'She was labouring?'

'Digging her garden ... but in dry weather, last Sunday. She was turning the soil before winter, lets the frost get down deep ... breaks up the soil, so it's better for planting in the spring, but Eddie, my husband, he works like that six days a week for Mr Styles. He's on the land.'

'Arthur Styles?'

'Yes, do you know him?'

'I've met him. I've come to know the people of this village quite well over the last few days. So, on Sunday you saw Nancy Braithwaite?'

'Yes, she was out there all afternoon. She could work, could Nancy, her and her dog.'

'Did you hear any commotion from her house in the last few days?'

'From quiet Nancy's house ... a commotion? Last time there was anything approaching a commotion was when she got sacked from the Manor House for stealing from the family there. She slammed the door of her house behind her and that was as close to a commotion you'd get from Nancy.'

'Didn't hear her dog ... what did you call him ... a prize terror? Didn't hear him barking at all?'

'No ... no more than usual, barks at the postman ... poor guy ... has to come all the way up Scrivener's Folly to deliver junk mail to Nancy ... she never gets personal mail.'

'How do you know?'

'Well, she's by herself, she has nobody in the world ... there's just her and her dog. So who would want to write to her? I mean, who?'

Hennessey made a mental note to check Nancy Braithwaite's letter basket inside her front door, but he had no reason to disbelieve her feisty neighbour.

'And the milkman ... at least he comes up Scrivener's Folly for a purpose.'

'Do you spend most of your time in the house?'

'Yes, that's what I am. Go out a bit into the village, but I am never away for more than an hour or so.'

'So a commotion could have occurred, just that you were out when it happened?'

'Yes, it could. Why?'

'I think you'll find out soon enough.'

'So, she's dead ... yes?'

Hennessey remained silent. The young woman's lack of concern, of care, chilled him.

'Well,' the woman continued, 'you break in, your mate calmly takes the dog away and the dog behaves like it's had an attitude transplant, you come here asking questions. If Nancy was talking, you'd be in *there* talking. If she was injured, you and your mate would be running round like a pair of headless chickens ... but you're not ... you're in here, your mate's taken Nancy's collie off somewhere, so Nancy's gone to a better place. Yes?'

'Perhaps,' Hennessey growled. 'Perhaps.'

'Well, what could be worse than this?'

'That's not what I meant. I meant perhaps in the sense I won't tell you. Like I said, you'll find out soon enough.' He turned and walked away. What the young woman had told him was intriguing, but he did not feel inclined to thank her.

He crossed Scrivener's Folly and knocked on the door of the cottage which stood opposite Nancy Braithwaite's cottage. The occupant revealed himself to be a man who, in Hennessey's mind, could best be described as jolly and, with what Hennessey thought to be unqualified appropriateness, that proved to be his name. Tom Jolly. Jolly by name, jolly by nature.

'She's a hard young woman.' Tom Jolly nodded to the cottage that Hennessey had just visited. 'Bet you didn't get any change out of her. I knew her mother, she was the same, all the Leddys are like that. Feel sorry for her husband, he's a nice lad from a good family. You'll be wanting to know about Nancy?'

'Yes.' Hennessey warmed to the man. He

was also short, but elderly, with wispy strands of grey hair on a balding head. A cairn terrier sat at his feet and, not very terrier-like, looked up at Hennessey with a wagging tail.

'He's my best pal–' Tom Jolly looked down at the terrier – 'but he's no guard dog, that's for sure. A stranger comes to the door – he wags his tail.'

Hennessey grinned. 'So, Nancy Braithwaite?'

'Monday night ... heard a bit of commotion ... her dog barking, which was unusual, but then it went quiet. Now her dog, that collie, he is a guard dog, Nancy was safe with him in her house, and if he went quiet quickly, then all was well, so I didn't pay any more attention, but come to think of it ... perhaps I should. It was unusual for Nancy to have visitors at all ... never at night ... and a countryman or a criminal would know how to quieten a dog: liquorice is best ... dogs will kill for liquorice. Give any guard dog tribute of a liquorice stick and he's your friend in an instant. I saw you and your friend force her door, the way you left ... calmly ... after your mate took her dog, that means there'll be a funeral to attend, I think?'

'I think you'll find you are right.'

Tom Jolly looked beyond Hennessey, at the trees on the skyline beyond the tilled fields. 'These are strange times for this village, first the family from the big house, and now Nancy. She used to work for them.'

'Yes, we know.'

'They said she stole from them, but Nancy wouldn't do that. I think they just wanted rid of her. They could have done it better ... let her go with a gesture of thanks, didn't have to accuse her of stealing.'

'So, Monday night ... what did you hear?'

'Voices ... male ... female.'

'Didn't recognize them ... the voices?'

'No, I didn't ... the woman's voice ... it wasn't Nancy's though.'

'That's interesting ... a man and a woman called on her. Did you hear anything that was said?'

'I didn't. Couldn't make out any words at all ... didn't sound angry though, so it's probably wrong to call it a commotion. It was just unusual for Nancy to have visitors.'

'They entered her house?'

'Yes ... some talking at the door–' Tom Jolly seemed to be recalling what he had heard – 'a silence, then the door shut, but the two people didn't walk away, otherwise I would have heard them in the lane. So the door must have been shut behind them.'

'What time was that, about?'

'Well, it was dark ... but this is November, gets dark about six ... but it was well after that ... not late ... probably eight ... probably nine.'

'Eight or nine,' Hennessey repeated, committing the time to memory. 'Did you hear them at all after that?'

'No. I don't stay up late, I go to my bed about ten every night. I don't go out at all after dark ... I'm too old, even though it is a safe village ... I am still too old, me and my pal are daytime walkers, aren't we?'

The terrier wagged its tail and placed a paw on Tom Jolly's foot, clearly, Hennessey noticed, responding to the word 'walkers'.

'Later, pal.' Tom Jolly spoke to his dog.

'So, I didn't hear anybody leave by ten p.m., and I sleep in the room at the back of my cottage ... not likely to hear anybody in the lane from my bedroom.'

'And nobody in or around Miss Braithwaite's cottage in this last week?'

'None that I saw.'

'You were not suspicious when you didn't see Miss Braithwaite at all?'

'Well...' Tom Jolly looked uncomfortable. 'It was unusual not to see her, that's fair, but the lights in her cottage went on when it got dark and went off late evening ... they must have been on timer switches. I'll be feeling guilty about that for some time now. I liked Nancy ... she was a good sort. Here's your mate.'

Hennessey glanced to his left and saw Yellich, who had tucked his trouser bottoms into his socks, making careful progress up Scrivener's Folly towards him.

'Well ... Mr...?' Hennessey turned to the elderly man.

'Jolly. Tom Jolly.'

'Mr Jolly ... if you should think of anything that may be of interest to us, you'll let us know?' Hennessey handed him a calling card.

'You're ... Mr Hennessey–' Jolly read the card – 'and this is the number to ring?'

'Yes and yes.'

'I don't have a phone, but there's a phone box in the village if I remember anything.'

'Well, thanks anyway, Mr Jolly.' Hennessey walked away from Tom Jolly's cottage and stood in the lane. When Yellich reached him, he said, 'Just done two house calls, immediate neighbours, those two cottages there.'

'Yes, boss.'

'Indications are that she was murdered on Monday evening ... voices were heard ... last confirmed sighting of her was the day before, seen digging her garden on Sunday last. One cottager heard her dog, the other didn't, but it seems to have been silenced quickly anyway.'

'How, boss? Chloroform, do you think?'

'Liquorice, I suspect.' And Hennessey told Yellich about liquorice and dogs.

'Well, the publican's a bit devastated, but he's looking after the dog and will hand it over to the animal welfare people ... just a question of waiting for the crew to arrive from Micklegate Bar.'

'They're here now.' Hennessey stepped to one side and raised his hand and, in response, the police van turned into Scrivener's Folly. It was followed by an unmarked van, which Hennessey knew contained the SOCOs, and the third vehicle he recognized as that which belonged to the police surgeon.

Hennessey led the police surgeon into

Nancy Braithwaite's cottage.

'Chilly,' Dr Mann remarked as he stepped over the threshold.

'I'm sorry?' Hennessey half-turned as he spoke.

'It's colder in the house than outside. Must be difficult to heat. I have come across such houses before.'

'Indeed. Well ... here, sir.' Hennessey indicated the corpse of Nancy Braithwaite.

Dr Mann, immaculately dressed, and turbaned as his religion dictated, knelt by the body. 'A formality in this case,' he said, 'but procedure has to be followed.' He stood. 'I confirm life extinct in this case at...' He glanced at his watch ... 'fourteen twenty-five hours, this day.'

'Fourteen twenty-five.' Hennessey wrote on his pad.

'And has been deceased a few days.'

'We think on Monday last,' Hennessey said. 'Going by witness reports.'

'Which is often just as accurate as anything a medical person can tell you.' He looked at the corpse just sitting there, no sign of violence. 'Head looks a bit limp, but that could be a natural position ... no sign of violence–' he looked about him – 'nothing out of place, nothing ransacked, but that's your department. All I can say is that life is extinct. You may move this into the next box.'

Hennessey smiled. 'Thank you ... into the next box it goes.'

Dr Mann walked out of the cottage. 'Nice to get out into the country for a change ... better than a stabbing in a snickelway.'

'Indeed,' Hennessey replied, walking out of the cottage behind Dr Mann. He approached Yellich and asked him to get on his 'brain-fryer' and request the attendance of Dr D'Acre. He then turned to the SOCO, who stood apart from the sergeant and the constables, the police culture not allowing them to mix with Scenes of Crime Officers, who are considered to be of a more lowly status. 'It's all yours,' he said. 'One female, deceased ... so we need photographs and latents. Many will belong to the deceased, but it's the ones that don't that we are interested in.'

'Very good, sir.' The SOCOs, three men and a woman, dressed in white coveralls, picked up their equipment and walked into the cottage.

'On her way, sir.' Yellich held up his mobile

as he approached Hennessey. He and Hennessey then proceeded to wait in silence, as did the constables and the sergeant, looking about them, looking at their feet, at the sky, seeming, like Dr Mann, glad to be out of the city for a change.

'We could be doing a house-to-house, boss.' Yellich broke the silence.

'Want to see if SOCO or Dr D'Acre turn anything up, then we'll do the house-to-house, and not just the cottages in the lane, we'll do the whole village. We'll knock on every door, don't care how long it takes, if—'

'Mr Hennessey!' a SOCO called from the door of the cottage and walked towards him. 'No information, sir,' he said when he stood with Hennessey and Yellich. 'I don't think we are going to find any alien latents in there, myself and our new trainee ... that's the young woman. We are dusting for prints, we keep coming across smooth finger marks.'

'Gloves?'

'Yes, sir. Two different types of glove ... one large, like a working glove, the other small, like a rubber glove used in dishwashing.'

'It's not exactly no information–' Hennessey smiled – 'it tells us something ... two people were in the house.'

'And they had a good rummage round, the glove prints are everywhere.'

'Which tells us they were looking for something.'

'Yes, sir. I thought you ought to know as soon as.' The SOCO was a middle-aged man who retained a youthful eagerness. Hennessey liked him. He turned and walked back to the cottage.

'Two people,' Hennessey said. 'One of the neighbours ... the old boy who lives in that cottage–' Hennessey indicated Tom Jolly's cottage – 'he said he heard a man and a woman call on Miss Braithwaite ... a male and a female voice, as I told you ... and nothing was stolen, nothing disturbed, yet they were looking for something ... and a link to the murders of the Inngey family.'

'A link?'

'She worked for the Inngeys.'

'Of course.' Yellich looked uncomfortable. 'Sorry, I wasn't thinking.'

'Yes,' Hennessey growled and the two men once again stood in silence, which both officers found a little more uncomfortable than the previous silence. It was broken by Yellich, who said, 'Dr D'Acre.' Hennessey turned and smiled as he saw Dr D'Acre's distinctive red and white Riley RMA turn into Scrivener's Folly and halt behind the police van. She got out of the car and was seen to be wearing a duffel coat over her green coveralls, and wellington boots upon her feet.

'You warned her about the conditions, I see,' Hennessey observed.

'Yes, boss.'

'For which she will doubtless be grateful.'

Louise D'Acre smiled as she approached Hennessey and Yellich. She greeted the two officers with a warm 'Good afternoon, gentlemen', and after pleasantries had been exchanged, Hennessey escorted her into the cottage.

'Her neck has been broken.' Dr D'Acre examined the corpse.

'Dr Mann made reference to the head seeming to be limp.'

'Yes, he was right to notice it ... rigor is well set in of course, but the limp look the head has is caused by a fracture of the spinal cord and the topmost vertebra, T-1 or T-2.' She stood. 'It is exactly the same sort of injury that was observed on the four corpses I examined earlier in the week. I'll venture there is a connection, though that is your department, of course, but I venture none-theless.'

'And you could be right, Dr D'Acre.' Hennessey smiled and held eye contact, but Louise D'Acre froze him with a glare and broke eye contact. 'She was a long-time employee of the Inngeys, and her house had been searched just like the Manor House, and just like the search of the Manor House, it appears to have been neat ... no ransacking ... and now you indicate that the cause of death was the same, so a strong connection indeed.'

'Well, it appears to be the same, only a post-mortem could tell us, but it does appear suspicious. I can do the PM tomor-row morning. Will you be representing the police?'

'Yes,' Hennessey nodded. 'This is my weekend off, but for this I'll come in.'

'It ought only to take up your morning, I don't anticipate any complications. I'll take a rectal temperature and an air temperature and collect any insect life, because I know that you'll want to know the time of death—'

she turned and smiled briefly – 'which we are not supposed to give but have allowed ourselves to be pressured into it.'

'Life imitating art, as you have so often said.'

'Yes … the cops on TV are given that information, so you real-life versions have come to expect it.'

'I suppose we have, but actually in this case, we have a pretty good idea when she was murdered. A witness recalls her being visited by two people on Monday evening.'

'Monday?' Louise D'Acre pondered the body; she sniffed the air. 'Damp … can't you smell it?'

'Yes.'

'Cold too … In this building, this body would have decayed as quickly as it would if left in the open … protected from scavengers … but would have decayed at the same rate … so four days ago … plus … yes, the impression is that of a four-day-old corpse. Well, I'll take those temperature readings, and if you have all the photographs you need, I'll arrange for her to be conveyed to York District Hospital.'

Yellich drove home. The mortuary van had

been summoned, the corpse of Nancy Braithwaite placed in a body bag and then stretchered into the van, observed by neighbours from behind net curtains. The front door of her cottage had been secured and a blue and white police tape strung across it, and also across the smaller rear door. Enquiries at all other homes on Scrivener's Folly had produced no new information. Dusk began to fall, the constables were soon to be needed in the Friday night city and so Chief Inspector Hennessey, in his words, decided to 'draw stumps' for the night. Yellich drove himself and Hennessey back to York, Nancy Braithwaite's emaciated dog, having been by then collected by the RSPCA. After leaving Hennessey at Micklegate Bar Police Station, he drove out of York to Huntington, and home.

As on many other occasions, as soon as Yellich arrived home, he was greeted by his son, who charged him with such force that Yellich had to brace himself for the impact, and also as on many other occasions, as soon as he arrived home, his wife grabbed her hat and coat and said she was 'going for a walk', that she had had him all day and that now it was 'his turn'.

Yellich then sat with his son, who, at twelve, could point to every letter in the alphabet and was beginning to master complicated times like 'twenty-two minutes to three' and was nearly able to tie his own shoelaces. With love, stability and stimulation, Jeremy Yellich could achieve a semi-independent living status by his early twenties, his own room in a hostel with cooking facilities so that he might prepare 'survival cooking' meals, but staff always on hand.

Later he and Sara sat side by side on the settee, listening to the music of Ralph Vaughan Williams and sharing a bottle of chilled Frascati.

'I should never have got married,' she said, putting her head against his, 'I should have remained Miss Medway, English teacher in the comprehensive ... I'd be head of the department now ... and I gave that up, all that up to become a police wife.'

Yellich squeezed her. 'You don't mean that.'

'No.' She laid her arm across his chest. 'I don't. I don't mean it at all.'

Six

... in which the investigation is further complicated and the gracious reader is privy to George Hennessey's other tragedy and present delight.

SATURDAY, 09.15 HOURS – 21.30 HOURS

Louise D'Acre pondered the body which lay face up on the stainless-steel table. Hennessey too looked at the body from where he stood at the edge of the room. Eric Filey similarly looked at the body and did so with a soberness which Hennessey thought unusual for him. Hennessey knew in himself that all three were thinking the same thing: that there was a sadness about the deceased in this instance. Some deaths, he felt, were a merciful release, but many are tragic, such as the needless death of someone in their prime. On this occasion though, the sadness was not associated with the death of Nancy Braithwaite, but her life. For there on the table was the body of a woman of late middle years who had led an eclipsed existence, believed to have lived in the same small village all her life, and who had struggled day by day to survive – the lines of worry were etched in her face, her fingernails were stumps, worn, not manicured, her hair was straggly and spoke of a dreadful self-image. She had worked in the 'big house' to care for her elderly father, before being dismissed, possibly unfairly, and had scratched pennies with no hope of release from poverty, and then had had her life taken prematurely from her. The lonely woman never had any visitors and then opened her door to two unexpected ones, who entered her small cottage, murdered her and then searched for something. Or vice versa. Probably the former, thought Hennessey, because no cries for help had been heard. Now she lay on the table, the requisite starched white towel covering her middle, and the three living persons in the room could not help but stare with feelings of poignancy and pity for the dead person. Thoughts of each were personal, 'There but for the grace of God', rather than detached and professional.

'The body is that of a middle-aged white European female.' Dr D'Acre focused the thoughts of Filey and Hennessey on to issues more practical. 'The corpse is reasonably well nourished ... she had a basic diet in life. There are no obvious injuries to the body, no cuts or contusions, but attention is drawn to the neck, and X-rays have shown that the spinal column was broken at the second vertebra. That was a deliberate act and in the absence of other injuries, such as those that could be sustained in a fall, means that it is non-accidental in nature. She was murdered. The body is showing signs of decay, which is not inconsistent with independent witness statements suggesting that she was murdered Monday last ... the nineteenth of November.' She turned to Hennessey. 'Have you confirmed her identity?'

'Her photograph is on a recently issued bus pass which SOCO found. It's Nancy Braithwaite all right. We don't think there is a next of kin.'

Louise D'Acre grimaced. She held eye contact with Hennessey but her facial expression was stern. 'No next of kin?'

'Not that we can tell. It will be up to social services to dispose of the body. They'll bury her in a common grave ... used to be called a pauper's grave ... three coffins in the same plot.'

'They don't cremate?'

'No, on the basis that if a relative does turn up, then she could always be cremated should the relative want that.'

'I see ... but you can't un-cremate someone in order to bury them. I can understand that ... terrible, lonely life.'

'Yes ... and aggravated by a sense of injustice at the end of it. She felt she had been wrongfully dismissed by her employers.'

'The Inngey link?'

'Yes.'

'Well...' Then turning back to the corpse, she spoke for the benefit of the microphone which was suspended above and to the front of her face on the end of a stainless-steel anglepoise arm. 'Can you give the name of this deceased as Nancy Braithwaite, please, Helen ... aged?' She turned to Hennessey.

'Sixty-one, going by the numbers on her bus pass.'

'Sixty-one years, thanks. Well, that certainly fits with the age of the appearance of the deceased–' Louise D'Acre examined the hands – 'and a hard-working sixty-one years at that.' Louise D'Acre leaned forward and examined the face of the corpse, forcing up an eyelid to expose the eye. 'Now that's interesting.'

Hennessey remained silent but his attention was total.

'Would you like to come and look at this, Detective Inspector?'

Hennessey padded silently across the industrial-grade linoleum floor, which was sealed with disinfectant, the green disposable paper coveralls he wore crumpling softly as he walked. He looked into the left eye of the deceased.

'See that?'

'I'm sorry, I can't see anything.'

'Well, the little pinpricks in the eye itself...'

'Oh yes...'

'Well, that's called petechial haemorrhages or "Taraiev's Spots" and is often associated with oxygen deprivation ... manual strangulation being the most common, but there is no bruising to the throat of the deceased. It can occur naturally if the deceased had heart disease or if the deceased died in a position where the head was lower than the body. But she was found sitting upright in a chair.'

'What could cause it? Other than strangulation or natural causes?'

'Well, as I said, some form of oxygen starvation ... but not all forms of oxygen starvation will cause it ... drowning or carbon monoxide or dioxide poisoning for example, is unlikely to cause it.'

'Suffocation?' Hennessey suggested.

'Possibly. It is unlikely, not as unlikely as drowning or atmospheric deprivation, but possible. A cushion held over her nose and mouth might ... just might cause it ... especially if she had a weak or diseased heart. And we can but see.' Dr D'Acre took a scalpel from the instrument trolley as Hennessey returned to the edge of the room.

Once again Dr D'Acre spoke for the benefit of the microphone. 'I am making a standard midline incision,' and drew the scalpel across the flesh to form a cut which looked like an inverted 'Y' on the chest of the corpse of Nancy Braithwaite, allowing the skin to be peeled back in three large folds. 'We'll see what her last meal was in a moment ... but first...' She placed the scalpel in a tray of disinfectant and picked up a compact electrical circular saw and switched it on. The machine made a high-pitched whining noise. She held the blade over the centre of the ribcage of the corpse, cracked what Hennessey had come to believe was her favourite joke about pathologists being the only doctors whose patients don't need anaesthetic and then applied the saw to the chest, separating the ribs down the centre. Deceased or not, the sight and sound made Hennessey wince. He noticed that Eric Filey too was looking very uneasy. The sawing completed, Dr D'Acre placed the saw on the instrument trolley, and using her hands, forced the ribcage open. The ribs cracked loudly as they 'gave'. She looked inside the ribcage. 'And here is your answer ... the heart has a pinker look ... looks more pink ... it indicates myocardial infarction.' She took the scalpel, severed the heart from the arteries, lifted it from the body and carried it to a set of scales. She placed the heart on the scales and said, 'Three hundred and forty grams is the weight of the heart,' again, clearly for the benefit of the microphone. She picked up the heart and placed it on a dissecting surface at the head of the dissecting table and, taking a large and clearly razor-sharp knife, began to slice the heart laterally into sections about five centimetres in width. She stopped when half of the heart had been thusly sliced. 'She had left ventricle failure.' She turned to Hennessey as she spoke. 'She could have gone at any time, but the condition of the heart would cause the petechial haemorrhaging if she was being suffocated.'

'Suffocation and a broken neck,' remarked Hennessey, 'somebody was making sure.'

'I am not sure she was killed by suffocation.' Dr D'Acre tapped her fingertips on the edge of the dissecting table. 'The petechial haemorrhaging is less marked than I would have expected had suffocation killed her, but it seems that some degree of suffocation was present ... but not fatally.'

'She was tortured?'

'It's a possibility.' Louise D'Acre turned to him. 'It's a grim possibility.'

Hennessey walked from York District Hospital back to Micklegate Bar Police Station and on a whim did not, as was his usual custom, walk the walls, rather opting for the Saturday thronged streets of shoppers and buskers and young people wrapped in blankets with a puppy on a length of string and a begging bowl in front of them. Some bowls, Hennessey noticed, even had a few coins inside them. He weaved his way up Micklegate, crossed the road and entered Micklegate Bar Police Station. He signed in and checked his pigeonhole. Just circulars. He left them to collect at a later date. He entered the CID corridor and walked to Yellich's office. He tapped on the frame of the door.

'Boss?' The look of surprise on Yellich's face rapidly gave to a diplomatic smile. 'Coming in on your day off ... dedication indeed.'

'Yes ... you busy?'

'Catching up with the paperwork.' He tapped a pile of files in front of him. 'All in a day in the life of a copper ... overworked, underpaid ... the burglaries in Tang Hall ... we have a good description of the window-turner...'

'Really?' Hennessey entered Yellich's office and sat in the chair in front of his desk. 'You don't mind?'

'Not at all, sir, it's quiet. The company is welcome. Tea?'

'Please.'

Yellich stood and walked to the corner of his office, where stood an electric kettle, a bag of tea, a carton of milk and an array of mugs. 'I presume you have just come from the post-mortem of Nancy Braithwaite?' He tested the kettle for its water content, and, satisfied, switched it on.

'Yes, broken neck, but signs of suffocation, though Dr D'Acre thinks the suffocation was not fatal.'

'Someone prolonging her death, trying to get information out of her?' He poured milk into each mug and added a teabag.

'That's what it looked like.' Hennessey adjusted his position in the chair. 'You see, that's why I came in ... didn't want to go home ... it's all too up in the air.'

'Do you want to kick it about?'

'If you don't mind?'

'Not at all, skipper, kick all you like.'

'The Inngeys and Nancy Braithwaite are connected.'

'Yes. Employee and employers.'

'Right. All appear to have been tortured

before being murdered.'

'Yes.' The kettle boiled. Yellich poured boiling water into the two mugs. 'The Inngeys were starved of food and Miss Braithwaite, you have just said, may or may not have been suffocated.'

'Right, as if to extract information.'

'They were all murdered in the same way.'

'Neck snapped asunder.'

Yellich walked back to his desk, handed Hennessey a mug of tea in a white-painted mug with a gold-embossed goat and the dates December 22nd – January 19th underneath. He sat at his desk cradling a mug which had a white rose on a blue background; underneath the emblem it read 'Yorkshire'. 'So a connection on two levels … the victims were known to each other, and the method of murder was the same. A broken neck.'

'So why torture someone?'

'To obtain information.' Yellich sipped his tea. 'Can't think of another reason.'

'To make someone confess, out of sheer sadism … but in this case, I think you are right. Whoever killed the Inngeys and their one-time maidservant wanted information. He/she/they believe they had information.'

'The mythical treasure trove,' Yellich said. 'Has to be really.'

'Couldn't obtain the information they wanted from the Inngeys, so they tried the maid. She didn't, or couldn't, come up with the goods, so she was cooled. Any feedback from the auctioneers yet?'

'None still ... I'll chase them up on Monday.'

'If it was the box of goodies they were after, it explains why the house was broken into. Someone believed, or knew, it existed. Tell me ... what do you think of leaving treasure like that in a ruin?'

'Not much,' Yellich smiled. 'Could have gone up in smoke ... all that wood panelling, all those floorboards would make a bonny blaze ... and when the rafters collapsed, it would destroy everything inside it.' He sipped his tea again, silently. Hennessey thought him to be well of manner. 'There is also the danger that it could have been found by a ruin-snooper, a ruin-snooper of the ilk of the man who found the bodies ... it's not an unknown pastime.'

'Ruin-snooping?'

'Yes. Illegal of course, but there's nothing to beat the thrill of exploring an old, large and deserted house ... room by room.'

'You sound as though you speak from experience, Sergeant Yellich,' Hennessey smiled.

'I do. Even police officers commit crime.'

'Don't tell me.'

'But this was when I was a lad of fourteen or so, and it wasn't really a ruin ... Halton House. I can see it and remember it now ... a large Victorian house, very generous gardens on a split level ... it was owned by the National Coal Board, as was, and had a caretaker family. It stood near to where I grew up ... anyway, the Coal Board deserted it.'

'Deserted?'

'Sold it and the land for redevelopment, and there was a summer when it stood empty. Me and my mates broke in and explored it ... I still remember it ... room by room ... long corridors, huge rooms. Honestly, you could have put my dad's house in one of the rooms. Like Edgefield House, it had been stripped out, just bare floorboards. We explored it from top to bottom, don't remember there being a cellar, but we went up into the attic. It wasn't boarded up, allowed us to see clearly when we were inside ... and that was a bit fatal.'

'Oh ... you didn't.'

Yellich smiled. 'I'm afraid we did ... every last window ... including the attic skylights.' He shrugged. 'Well, we knew it was going to be demolished, explains why it was easy to break in. It had no value any more. Lovely house though, crying shame to demolish it, had another hundred and fifty years of life in it. Newly-built residential home for frail elderly on the site now ... also called Halton House ... so it survives in name at least. But I have longed to find another such house ... one that is empty, but not dangerous to wander in. It remains a fancy of mine. I wouldn't do it, but only because I am now a serving police officer, but the lure of large, empty, accessible, and above all old buildings which are ripe for exploration, is difficult to resist and I find it remarkable that that chest of goodies was not found by a ruin-snooper.'

'So for two reasons you find it difficult to believe that that treasure was deliberately left where we found it?'

'I find it incomprehensible, boss.' He swallowed his tea.

'So do I.'

'What can you deduce from that?'

'That if the Inngeys knew it was there, they are more insane than they were believed to be ... a mad family ... but madder than realized, or, more probably, that they didn't know it was there.'

'I would think the latter.'

'Just left when a previous generation of family turned the key and walked out of Edgefield House. Still in the family by the way, the Land Registry came back to us on that one. As did the DNA results ... the buccal swab from Harold Inngey's mouth confirms the identities of the deceased as being Patrick, Victoria, Percy and Anne Inngey. There was really no doubt, but the confirmation of the DNA seals it. We got both results in the mail this forenoon.'

'Yes ... agreed...' Hennessey drained his mug and placed it on Yellich's desk. 'The confirmation is reassuring, but the doubt was minimal anyway.'

Hennessey looked at Yellich, holding eye contact. He raised his eyebrow.

'Little Miss Hewlett?' Yellich suggested.

'I think so. Let's look at her statement again. She admits looking for the chest in a half-hearted way, but nonetheless she admits looking for it.'

'And seemed keen to point the accusing finger at the wayward son, the man with the van who is now Lord Inngey and may be in possession of a fortune, depending on the valuation of the contents of the chest.'

Yellich and Hennessey drove out to Dringhouses. Yellich spoke as he halted the car beside Samantha Hewlett's house. 'You don't mind giving up your day off, skipper?'

'I'm not giving all of it up,' Hennessey smiled. 'I have plans for later on ... but I am at a loose end right now. So no, I don't mind.'

The two officers got out of Yellich's car and walked up the drive to Samantha Hewlett's house. The front door was ajar. Both officers noted it, both thought it strange, both knew the other had seen it and both knew what the other was thinking. They reached the front door and glanced at each other.

'Don't like the look of this.' Hennessey pushed the door open a little, sufficient to enable him to look into the hallway. All seemed normal.

Yellich pressed the doorbell. 'Better

announce our presence.'

The bell echoed inside the house. There was no response.

'Miss Hewlett,' Hennessey called out. As with the doorbell, his voice elicited no response. He turned to Yellich. 'Folk don't leave their front door open, and especially not in weather like this.'

'Sara certainly wouldn't, loses all the central heating, sends the bills sky-high ... I mean ballistic.'

'I can imagine. Miss Hewlett!' Hennessey paused. He pushed the door fully open. 'We'd better go in.'

She had put up a tremendous struggle. That was plain. There had at least been a violent fight in the living room of the house, so much so that no item seemed to be in its rightful place and if it was, it was smashed. The officers toured the house, moving carefully, remaining with each other. No other room seemed to have been disturbed. Whatever had happened had happened in the living room.

'And in the evening too,' Hennessey said.

Yellich glanced at him.

'Curtains in that room are drawn shut.'

'Ah...'

'And being at the back of the house, it wouldn't be seen. The front-room curtains shut would look a bit "iffy" during the day ... but who's to see the back-room curtains, one or two neighbours, if that? We'd better get SOCO here and a team of constables.'

Yellich took his mobile out of his pocket and jabbed the number of Micklegate Bar Police Station with his right middle finger. After he had relayed the request, he and Hennessey retraced their steps out of the house and sat sheltering from the rain in Yellich's car.

'So–' Hennessey wound down the window of his side of the car to prevent the windscreen and windows misting up – 'what have we got?'

'A mystery.'

'Well ... four members of the same family ... and we'll be charitable and say they were eccentric.'

Yellich smiled. 'That's very charitable, skipper ... they were mad.'

'All right, a mad, screwball family ... found murdered in an old and derelict house which they owned but did not live in. They had been starved of food before they were murdered by having their necks broken.'

'OK.' Yellich wiped the windscreen. 'That takes some skill.'

'Yes ... and the one member of the family who is still alive and possesses that skill is Harold, ex-Royal Marine Commando, and now the sole inheritor of the family fortune. He's not out of the frame yet, Yellich, not by a long chalk.'

'No, boss.'

'Then we find that the rafters of the old house sheltered a box of goodies, still to be valued, but family rumour has it that it contained wealth ... real wealth ... and a search has been made for it, by Harold and Miss Hewlett, and also a search had been made of the Manor House at Long Hundred ... damn strange place that village ... damn strange. So somebody was looking for something.'

'The rumoured family treasure?'

'Has to be.' Hennessey put his hands together, intertwined his fingers and twiddled his thumbs. 'And then a long-serving employee of the family is found in her cottage, her neck also broken. And now...' he nodded to Samantha Hewlett's house, 'Miss Hewlett appears to have been a victim of violence, and appears to have disappeared.'

'Hell of a mess in the living room ... must have been a terrific scrap. She went down fighting.'

'She is a Thai kick-boxing champion.'

'Really?' Yellich glanced at Hennessey.

'Yes, really. She could have handled herself. So who could have overpowered a girl who can kick-box her way out of a rammy?'

'An ex-Royal Marine?'

'You're not letting Harold Inngey go, are you, boss?'

'Nope,' Hennessey smiled. 'And the door wasn't forced. She knew the person who attacked her. And those two were as thick as thieves once ... and you can never unstick yourself from a person once you've been involved, not fully.'

'But for what motive?'

'To be answered, Yellich, to be answered, but we have five murder victims and one person who has apparently disappeared and all of the same family, or linked with it. There's a term for this in the trade, Yellich.'

'Oh?'

'Yes ... it's called a can of worms ... Ah, here we are.'

Yellich glanced ahead of him and saw the dark SOCO van, following a police van, turn into the road. He and Hennessey got out of his car, turning their collars up against the rain as they did so. The police vehicle halted by the kerb and a uniformed sergeant stepped out. He didn't wear a cape and seemed not to notice the rain. 'Mr Hennessey,' he said.

'Thank you for coming so promptly.' Hennessey smiled briefly at the sergeant. 'This house here.'

'Yes, sir.'

'The door was found ajar by myself and Mr Yellich here.'

'I see, sir.'

'We entered it ... found the occupant missing and signs of a fierce struggle having taken place.'

'I see, sir.'

'The house owner is linked to the Inngey family.'

'The multiple murder?'

'Yes. We wanted to talk to her, hence our calling on her, and we found what we found. So we want the house searched thoroughly, you know the drill, in the attic, in the crawl space beneath the floorboards, every cupboard, and any shed in the back garden ... and the garage ... if it's big enough to

230

contain a body, open it up.'

'Very good, sir.'

'Then, only when you are satisfied that there is no body in the house, ask SOCO to do their stuff, photograph every room and dust for latents. Mr Yellich and I will be house-to-housing.'

'Understood, sir.' The sergeant turned and opened the door of the police van, which Hennessey saw contained four male and two female officers. 'Right, lads and lassies,' he said, 'the Chief Inspector has a job for you'.

Hennessey and Yellich walked up the drive of the adjoining semi-detached house. Hennessey rang the doorbell. He turned to Yellich. 'The dividing wall between these houses is only one line of bricks thick. If anybody heard something, this household would.'

'Aye.' The elderly gentleman seemed un-interested. 'Heard quite a rumble in the night.'

'Last night?' Hennessey asked.

'Aye.' The man looked beyond Hennessey and Yellich at the police and SOCO vehicles.

'You didn't think to call the police?'

The man shrugged. 'We don't like each

other, me and the young woman ... Hewis ...
Hewlett ... whatever her name. She's noisy,
that music, and she often has arguments
with men, furniture gets smashed, cups get
thrown, so nothing new about noise from
her house, nothing new at all.'

'This must have been more than just an
argument,' Hennessey growled, dispirited at
the man's evident lack of concern for his
youthful neighbour's welfare.

'Well, I am a bit Mutt and Jeff–' the man
pointed to his ear – 'and it didn't go on for
long, only a minute or two.'

'As little as that?'

'Well, what I heard ... but like I said...' He
indicated his ear again. He was about sixty,
Hennessey thought, be-whiskered and of
unkempt appearance. He could see why he
and Samantha Hewlett saw little to like in
each other as neighbours. 'And I keep the
television turned up loud so I can hear it ...
and I can still hear her music, that's how
loudly she plays it. No thought for others,
not like old Mrs Small who had the house
before she did. Now, that was a good neighbour, quiet as a church mouse, kept herself
to herself, kept her garden neatly. Not like
little Miss what's-her-name, who seems to

get whichever man she's in tow with to hack it back into place for her.'

'So what time did you hear the commotion?'

'About ten o'clock last night. It didn't last long ... about two minutes, then it went quiet again.'

Hennessey felt that that was a more acceptable excuse for not phoning the police. He could understand the man's reluctance to do so, just two minutes of scuffling, then silence ... And, in fairness, a room *could* be wrecked in the space of 120 seconds.

'Did you see anything?'

'Of her?'

'Or anything that was out of the ordinary?'

'A van, parked outside her house. It arrived just before the commotion.'

'A van?'

'Yes ... a bit like the police van except it had no windows, just plain sides.'

Hennessey glanced at Yellich. 'A van,' he said. Yellich nodded. 'Seen the van before?'

'Possibly ... she had a fancy man who drove one, same sort of shape, same dark colour.'

'Could you say whether it was the same van?'

The man shrugged. 'It might have been ... I wouldn't swear it was, it was dark and raining. I just glanced out of my window, by then it was quiet and there was a news item I wanted to watch.'

'You were watching the news?'

'Yes ... the BBC *News at Ten*.'

'And during that programme you heard the sound of a commotion from Miss Hewlett's home?'

'Yes.'

'And you mentioned a news item?'

'The trial of the corrupt councillors ... it's at York Crown Court at the moment.'

'Yes.'

'So I turned away from the window when I heard the newscaster announcing that news item. I knew one or two of them, you see.'

'You knew them?'

'Aye ... I used to be a town councillor and a magistrate, they were never friends of mine, but I knew them ... three of them, always thought they were a shifty bunch.'

'I see. So, if we were to contact the BBC, they could tell us to the minute when the news item about the corrupt council members was broadcast, that would enable us to pin down the time of the violence in Miss Hewlett's house to within a matter of minutes.'

'Dare say it would.' The man's attitude continued to be uninterested.

'I'll do that, boss,' Yellich offered.

'If you would. Might be handy to have it pinned down to within a minute or two.' Hennessey turned to the man. 'You didn't see or hear anything after that?'

'No ... nothing out of the ordinary.'

'What time did the van leave?'

'Don't know.'

'You don't know?'

'No, I don't know. It was still there when I turned in for the night at eleven thirty p.m. I sleep lightly but the old hearing...' Again his hand went up to his ears. 'I hear even less at night than I do during the day. Anyway, it was gone when I woke up this morning.'

'I see ... Now the commotion ... were you able to pick out any sounds?'

'Just her shouting and screaming ... things being thrown.'

'Interesting. Did you hear anybody else's voice?'

'There was a man's voice and a woman's.'

'A man's voice and a woman's?'

'Seemed like it,' the man nodded. 'Yes ... I heard one male voice, seemed gruff and rough ... and a female ... but the female only screamed. I didn't hear the female say anything as such, but she screamed as the furniture went flying. Then it went silent. Then I looked out the front, saw the van parked up against the kerb in the rain and then the news item about the bent councillors came on and so I went back to the television.'

'Well, thanks.' Hennessey spoke reluctantly. It was clear to him that the man should have called the police, but he could equally understand his hesitation – there was, he had noticed about humans, an unwillingness to interfere in such circumstances. Things seemed to him to have to be extreme before neighbours would involve themselves with each other. 'If you should remember any other detail...' Hennessey handed him a calling card with his name and phone number printed on it.

'DCI Hennessey.' The man read the card.

'Yes, and you are?'

'Small. Norbert Small.'

'Small? Your late neighbour's name, quite

a coincidence.'

'No coincidence.' A sour note entered the man's voice. 'She was my sister. We never married but bought these two houses, one part of a semi, each ... we were quite close, went out together a lot ... folk used to say we were joined at the hip. They weren't being unkind, it's just that we'd do our shopping together, and things like that. She was my little sister ... ten years younger than me. She was killed in a road accident ... a motor-cyclist roaring down the street as she was crossing the road ... Never did like those machines, now I hate them, and I sold my own car after that, five years ago. She'd be just fifty-two now, if she had lived.'

'I'm sorry,' Hennessey said, but he knew what Norbert Small meant, oh, didn't he know ... didn't he know.

Hennessey and Yellich walked away from Norbert Small's door. As they did so, the police sergeant walked out of Samantha Hewlett's house. The officers glanced and nodded to each other and met on the pavement midway between the two houses.

'Nothing in the house, sir,' the sergeant said. 'We are satisfied ... we've conducted a thorough search ... attic, crawl space, and every little nook and cranny in-between ... no body, alive or dead, is in that house, save for our boys.'

'Thanks, Sergeant. Did you see or find anything that might be suspicious, in your view?'

'In my view, sir, no, nothing ... except for the wrecked living room. Oh ... nothing in the garden shed or the garage either.'

'Thanks again. I'll ask SOCO to go in and photograph the interior and dust for prints. We'll continue our house-to-house, so if we are needed, we'll be in the immediate vicinity.'

'Next of kin, sir?' Yellich prompted. 'We should inform them ... it seems she has been abducted ... they should be informed.'

'Yes...' Hennessey's voice trailed off. Yellich of course was correct. That oversight had been careless. 'Can you see to that, Yellich? Look for an address book ... you know the form.'

'Very good, sir.'

'I'll continue with the house-to-house.'

Hennessey's enquires at households in the immediate vicinity of Samantha Hewlett's house, five on either side, and all the houses on the opposite side of the road, brought no new information. None of the householders had seen anything, one or two thought they might have heard an argument but that was nothing remarkable they said, not from *that* house. Half an hour later Hennessey and Yellich sat in Yellich's car as Yellich thumbed through Samantha Hewlett's address book. 'Popular girl was Samantha.'

'Was?' Hennessey glanced sideways at him.

'All right ... is, don't want to anticipate the worst. Sorry, boss, you're right.'

'But she's in trouble.' Hennessey glanced out of the window at Norbert Small's house. What the man had said had struck a chord deep within him. 'She's disappeared ... apparently after putting up a fight with a man and a woman ... taken against her will, and she's linked to a case where there are just too many dead bodies ... five at the last count. And that's five that we know of.'

'That we know of.' Yellich echoed Hennessey's words. 'Here we are ... looked under "M" for "Mum and Dad" ... looked under "D" for "Dad and Mum" ... looked under "P" for "parents" ... found it under "U" for "uncle". It's the nearest there is.'

'Back to Long Hundred?'

'Yes ... how did you know?'

'She told me it was her home village, remembers Harold Inngey when she was a little lassie.'

'I see. Do you want me to do this, boss?' Yellich put Samantha Hewlett's address book on the rear seat of his car. 'This is your day off.'

'Got no plans till this evening anyway, so it's all right.'

'Oh ... going out?' Yellich turned the ignition key.

'No ... no, I'm staying in, expecting a guest for dinner.'

'Ah...'

The drive out to Long Hundred was undertaken in silence, which suited Hennessey – his thoughts had been triggered by Norbert Small. As Yellich drove smoothly and calmly out of York and across the Vale, Hennessey's thoughts turned to his elder brother, Graham, who had also died by motorbike, though as a rider. As with Jennifer, as he had gone through life with its succession of achievements, setbacks and further tragedy and delights, Hennessey had often wondered what his elder brother would have been like. What would he have been like in his twenties, his thirties, his forties, his fifties...? Now he would have been a man in his sixties, retired, possibly with grandchildren. Hennessey pondered what Graham would have done in his life ... Whatever it was it would have been something positive, of that he was certain ... The world, he believed, would have been a better place for Graham Hennessey having been in it. The unfairness about the motorcyle accident was that the machine had been a passing phase in his life ... for some weeks before his death he had more than once mentioned selling the bike and buying a car – much to his parents' relief. Hennessey felt that had Graham's life been dedicated to motorbikes, then his death would have been easier to bear and he would have died doing what he most loved ... but it was by then evident that despite the Triumph being his pride and joy it was a passion which had begun to evaporate. Graham was talking of his future, of giving up his lowly position at the bank and training to become a photojournalist ... He would look at photographs published in newspapers of events in war zones and would say, 'That's the sort of photograph I want to take ... that sort of photograph can bring things home to people and stop things happening...' Not for Graham Hennesey would have been the trendy chic of glamour or fashion photography ... put a camera in his hands, put him in the right place at the right time and Graham Hennessey would have brought change for the better. Hennessey believed his brother would have become that sort of man. From the moment of Graham's death, Hennessey had grown to dislike motor vehicles, whether of two wheels or four, believing them to be the most dangerous machines ever invented, killing well over three thousand people a year in the UK alone. He drove a car because he had to, and only when he had to. And then, as always when at work with another officer, he was content to let the other officer do the driving.

Yellich turned off the greasy, mud-bespattered main road and entered the village of Long Hundred and muttered, 'Home sweet home ... getting to be a habit coming here.' He halted the vehicle outside the small shop, telling Hennessey he was obtaining directions. He returned a few minutes later and said, 'Cottage near the post office ...

white door.' He started the vehicle, drove slowly along the road with the line of cottages on one side and the green with the duck pond on the other, and halted by a cottage with a white door.

'Rose Cottage.' Hennessey read the name beside the door and pondered the fact that only very small or very large dwellings have sufficient character to allow themselves to be named, and how silly names look on houses in suburbia.

'Aye.' Yellich switched off the engine.

The officers got out of the car and Yellich tapped on the black-painted knocker, tap, tap ... tap and again, Hennessey was transported back to the agony and the injustice of his distinct eighth year ... that same police officer's knock heralding as it did the news of Graham's death.

The white door opened slowly. A middle-aged woman peered at the two officers, blinking as she did so. 'Aye?' Her hair was in curlers, she wore an ill-fitting cardigan over a sack like dress. Her feet were encased in solid black shoes ... only an extra inch on the heel said that they were women's shoes.

'Mrs Hewlett?'

'Aye.'

'Police.' Hennessey and Yellich showed their IDs.

'There's trouble...' The woman suddenly seemed close to tears. 'Adam,' she called behind her, 'Adam.'

A fumbling and stumbling and crashing was heard from within the cottage and a white-haired man came and stood behind Mrs Hewlett. He too blinked at the officers and he too said, 'Aye?'

'May we come in?' Hennessey asked.

'What's it about?'

'You have a niece, Samantha?'

'Aye.'

'I think you'd better let us come in, we have some news for you ... which ... well, it's not the worst, but it's not good either.'

'Aye...' The man and woman stepped aside and Hennessey and Yellich entered Rose Cottage.

It was, thought Hennessey, cramped inside but it was certainly warm and dry, quite 'cosy' in a word. A coal fire crackled in a stone fireplace, brasses hung on the walls, as did inexpensive prints of hunting scenes. The smoke-blackened wooden mantelpiece contained photographs of Samantha Hewlett ... many in a gym in kick-boxing attire.

'So what's happened?' Mr Hewlett held his wife. She held him.

'Well, are you Samantha's next of kin? We understood her father died ... is her mother still alive?'

'No ... she's not ... and so yes, we are Samantha's next of kin.'

'No sisters or brothers?'

'She was an only child.'

'I see ... well, it seems Samantha has disappeared.'

'Disappeared?' Mrs Hewlett gasped. 'But she phoned us yesterday.'

'What time was that?'

'About five or six, yesterday evening.'

'Well, we have a fairly reliable witness who informs us that a commotion was heard inside Samantha's house later yesterday evening, about ten o'clock, shortly there-after in fact ... and I also have to inform you that her house ... the living room ... showed signs of violence.'

'Violence! But Samantha can take care of herself ... she's a kick-boxer ... that's her, all those photographs, she's got medals and cups and such like.'

'Do you see much of Samantha?'

'Well ... enough for us ... you know she

visits. We never had children and we used to take her on holiday with us ... she got two summer holidays ... lucky lassie. She always said it was like having two sets of parents ... double the amount of presents each Christmas. Then, when she lost her parents ... my brother died in an accident, her mother went soon after ... that just left me and Alice, so she'd keep in touch.'

'You were quite close to her in that case?'

'Aye ... you could say that. She is a good girl, isn't she, Adam?'

'Did she tell you what she was doing? Who she was associating with?'

'She was looking for work, I can tell you that...'

'What about friends?'

'We don't know her friends in York ... just her friends in the village.'

'We understood she knew Harold Inngey?'

'Aye ... they had a bit of a thing between them.'

Adam Hewlett sounded disapproving of the union. Hennessey remarked on it. 'Well, it's not just that the Inngeys are a strange family ... but they're not like us ... our class. I'm a farm labourer, Samantha's father was the same ... she's a farm-worker's lassie ...

246

and they–' he nodded in the direction of the Manor House – 'well, they were titled folk.'

'What about her friends in the village here?'

'Just the doings she had with the Styles family.'

'The Styleses? The farmer who owns the land next to the Manor House?'

'He rents it, but yes, that's him, she seemed to have dealings with him.'

'Not like a relationship,' Alice Hewlett said. 'There was quite an age gap, but he became well keen to get to know our Samantha once she took up with Harold Inngey ... but other than that, I don't know of anyone else she knew, do you, Adam?'

Driving back to York, Hennessey broke the silence by saying, 'I think we'd better have another word with Harold Inngey.'

'I think we had, boss.' Yellich kept his eyes firmly on the road. 'I think we had. Got time pressure on us now ... if that girl is still alive, well, we have time pressure now.'

Yellich drove to Simcock Avenue on the Broadwood Estate. The officers saw Harold Inngey's van parked outside number twenty-three.

'He's home.' Yellich slowed the car.

'Possibly,' Hennessey growled, 'only possibly.'

Less than five minutes later, they were certain he was not at home.

'He's keeping her somewhere.' Yellich seemed to Hennessey to be angry, more angry than he had seen him. 'She's not in there–' he pointed to the house – 'she won't be in the van.'

Hennessey did not reply, but taking his mobile from his pocket, he phoned Micklegate Bar Police Station. 'Same request as earlier today,' he said, 'except we don't know whether we need SOCO. I'll call you back on that one.'

Yellich looked questioningly at him.

'We won't know until we have looked in, either,' he said. 'If that young woman is being held against her will, I am going into that house and then into that van. I am not hanging about for niceties ... when the boys get here, that door's opening. Meanwhile, see what you can do with your car keys with that van's doors ... a little bit of gentle teasing ... the wrong keys have opened the right lock before now.'

Yellich nodded. 'You've got it, boss.' He turned and walked towards the van. He returned moments later. 'Plenty of junk, but no Miss Hewlett. Didn't think there'd be.'

'I didn't think so either, but I'm pleased we checked.'

A sergeant and four constables arrived at the house. Hennessey pointed to the back door and said, 'Put it in.' The door went 'in' alarmingly easily, the wood surrounding the lock, upon examination by a curious George Hennessey, revealing itself to be rotten. But more importantly, in Hennessey's view, the small semi-detached council house proved itself to be unoccupied by either Harold Inngey or by the missing Samantha Hewlett.

'Where now?' Yellich appealed to Hennessey.

'Home for me,' Hennessey said. 'For you ... secure this door as best you can, leave a police card inside, then get back to the station, contact the media ... better make the abduction as high-profile as we can ... appeal for witnesses. You know what's required.'

'Yes, boss.'

'Then wait. It's the hardest thing to do ... nothing is the hardest thing to do ... but do it. If it was a child, it would be different, you know that, but it's not, it's an adult, so we can't do anything. We can't do anything, not until we get a break.'

'Surely,' Yellich appealed to Hennessey, 'there must be something?'

'Well, if you think of something, by all means do it. Take me back to the station, please.'

Hennessey drove home. His stomach felt hollow and empty at the same time. He could well understand Somerled Yellich's anxiety: the likelihood that Samantha Hewlett had been abducted was real, the likelihood was further that her abduction was in some way connected to the murder of the Inngey family ... but what to do ... how to be proactive? That was the question. The question plagued his journey home but upon approaching his house, his heart lifted ... for there parked half on and half off the kerb was a silver BMW. He slowed and turned into his driveway. The sound of his car brought forth an excited barking from Oscar. It also brought forth a younger man who exited his house, smiling as he walked towards Hennessey. Hennessey left his car and the two men shook hands warmly before going inside.

'Not got them all yet?'

'Sorry?' Hennessey turned away from the electric kettle and saw the younger man reading the list of names.

'No, just five elude me ... same names barked out each schoolday morning for five years ... you'd think I'd remember them. I know the form fluctuated in size from twenty-nine at its least to thirty-three at its greatest number ... but those five.'

'They'll come, Dad.'

'Oh, I am sure they will ... in time.' Hennessey poured the boiling water into the teapot, stirred the contents and allowed them to settle.

'So how are things, work-wise? Family-wise?'

'Work-wise ... well, I'm in Teesside all next week ... I was there all last week, my man insists on going N.G. to murder ... the weight of evidence is monumental, but he definitely did not do it.' Charles Hennessey smiled. 'I tried to persuade him to change his plea to guilty to manslaughter. I'm sure the Crown would accept that.'

'He would still get life.' Hennessey poured the tea and carried the two mugs over to the table.

'Yes, but with a lower parole tariff ... it would be a better deal for him. He could be out in ten years ... but he won't be advised ... he has convinced himself that he's innocent and that's that. At the end of the day, all we can do is act upon his instructions. This is one I won't get off. You've caught this one and he'll stay caught. He's young too ... just twenty-two ... heavens, if he'd only go G. but he's insisting on going Not Guilty. He'll be in his forties before he walks and breathes free air again ... if he took advice, he'd be out when he's still got a lot of his youth left.'

'But they won't.' Hennessey wrapped his meaty hands round his mug. 'I know the type.'

'And family ... very well ... children anxious to see granddad again and getting excited about Christmas.'

'Already!'

'Already ... still nearly two months to go and they are talking about it.' Charles Hennessey sipped his tea too. 'So what's happening with *you* work-wise? Socially?'

'Well ... work ... I have the Inngey case.'

'You've got that! Saw the news, I wondered if that was one of yours.'

'Well, it is ... and it took a turn for the worse today, a woman on the edge of the case has disappeared ... it has to be connected, it just has to be.'

'Prime suspect?'

'One ... we quizzed him once but he's not at home, but the van's there.'

'The van?'

'Used to abduct the woman ... a van was seen parked outside her home at the time she was abducted. Her ex-partner has a van and there is ill feeling between them.'

'Mmmm...' Charles Hennessey smiled wryly at his father. 'Not what the law would accept as proof of identity.'

'Long way to go yet, but it's our only lead.'

'And socially?'

'Oh quiet ... the Dove Inn pretty well every evening ... and Oscar.'

'And your lady friend? I am anxious to meet her.'

'I think she'd like to meet you too ... you must come over ... I'll arrange it.'

Later, Oscar having been fed and exercised and left with sufficient food and water and with access to a safely fenced-off garden via the dog flap in the back door, George Hennessey turned a deaf ear to his dog's high-pitched barks of protest and, with an overnight bag packed, he drove from Easingwold to Skelton, to a half-timbered house. He parked his car at the kerb and walked up the gravel drive. He rang the doorbell. The door was opened rapidly upon his ringing of the bell. The homeowner smiled a welcoming smile and slipped a welcoming arm round his neck, as he kissed her.

'Sorry I am a little late,' he said. 'I went in this morning and caught up on things and Charles was there when I got home.'

'No matter.' Louise D'Acre pushed the door to behind him. 'The children are with their father ... we've got all evening and all tomorrow until six o'clock.'

Seven

... in which Yellich is reckless.

SATURDAY, 16.00 HOURS – MONDAY,
09.30 HOURS

Proactive. That was the word. Proactive,
proactive, proactive. Yellich clenched his fist
and thumped the desk. The police should be
more proactive on this one. He glanced out
of his office window: the sky was low and
grey, the rain had by then stopped falling,
but more seemed to be threatened. And
somewhere out there was a young woman
who was being held against her will. He
believed Hennessey to be wrong: It isn't, he
thought, good enough to wait until something 'breaks'; he believed that decisive
action had to be taken. But what action
could he take? He leaned back in his chair.
What action was there to take? Once again

255

he glanced out of the window ... there was about two perhaps three hours of daylight left – any action, he reasoned, would have to be done before dusk. He stood and paced the floor in front of his desk. It occurred to him that the key to the case might not be people, not people at all, but *place*. The more he thought, the more he became convinced that the key was in the strange inward-looking village of Long Hundred. Without knowing specifically why, he decided to drive out there. He clambered into his coat and swept his car keys off the surface of his desk and signed out to 'Long Hundred – returning about 6.00 p.m.'. He intended to walk round the village ... just stroll round it ... perhaps there was something to be noticed, something that the police with their focus on the Manor House and Nancy Braithwaite's cottage had not noticed, but which was hugely significant. Half an hour's drive at a modest speed took him to the village. He parked his car by the small shop and, aware of people in the shop looking at him, he began to stroll round the village which he saw again was laid out like a 'V' with a green area between the two lines, the Manor House lying just beyond the point of the 'V' and housing beside the two lines of the 'V'. He walked down the left-hand side of the village, with cottages to his left, and the green with the duck pond to his right. As when he and Hennessey had first visited the village, there was no one in sight: just he alone was walking; the only other living things in the immediate vicinity being ducks on the pond. But as with the people in the shop, he became aware of people looking at him from within cottages: a curtain flicked as he passed; his eye was caught by movement to his right from within a house at the far side of the green but, when he turned, the figure, if that was what it was, had disappeared from view. He suddenly realized that many pairs of eyes were upon him. It was, he sensed, a very secretive village, a very defensive village, very suspicious of strangers. A village, he thought, with something to hide. He walked past Rose Cottage and pondered Adam and Alice Hewlett fretting for the safety of their niece. It seemed pointless to call on them. He carried on walking, a slow, deliberate police officer's walk and, reaching the point of the 'V' that was the street plan of Long Hundred, he walked up the further side of the village, past Scrivener's Folly, at the end of which stood Nancy Braithwaite's cottage, now deserted, and doubtless soon to be re-let.

The Inngeys, he thought, first the Inngeys ... four of them, one son survived ... then Nancy Braithwaite ... all with their necks snapped ... now Samantha Hewlett had disappeared. All lived in this village, or had lived here ... and the break-in at the spartan Manor House ... by some person or persons clearly in search of something. And the one man who seemed to be at the core of this web had disappeared, although unlike Miss Hewlett, his disappearance did not at that point seem sinister. Curtains continued to flick as he walked past them. On the far side of the green, a woman glanced at him nervously as she left the shop and walked hurriedly away, nearly running, clearly anxious to reach the corner of the street, and the gap in the line of cottages, into which she darted.

Fear. Yellich sensed then that Long Hundred was also a frightened village. Somebody, possibly some few people, knew something which they didn't want to tell the police, or were too fearful to tell the police. He continued walking and reached the Three Horseshoes. He went in. Saturday afternoon: the pub was more occupied than when he and Hennessey had visited. As he stepped into the lounge, the conversation stopped, eyes turned to look at him, then the hum of conversation resumed. He went to the bar.

'Hello again,' the landlord greeted him with false good humour. Yellich sensed clear hostility beneath the warmth.

'I'd like to talk to your brother.'

A look of fear flashed across Styles's eyes. It was there for an instant, but it was there.

The hum of conversation stopped. It didn't start again. All ears were clearly on Yellich and the landlord of the Three Horseshoes – Yellich knew he had struck a chord.

There was the sound of dominoes being shuffled but no other noise.

'Why?' The landlord's manner was no longer good humoured. It was icy: menacing.

'Just like to ask him a few questions,' Yellich answered slowly, deliberately. 'He lives close to the Manor House. We just wonder if he might have seen something.'

'We?'

'The police.'

A domino was placed on a table, a match was struck.

'He's not under suspicion?'

'No. Should he be?'

Arnold Styles didn't reply. His eyes remained icy.

'So ... directions to Arthur Styles's farm, please.'

'Bottom of the village. Lane to the left, last lane before you leave the village proper. Five Oaks Farm. Can't miss it.'

'Thanks.' Yellich nodded and smiled and left the pub. He walked towards the bottom of the village, following the directions he had been given and did so with the sense that he had stirred a hornets' nest. This perhaps was the 'break' his more cautious senior officer was waiting for. Yellich felt pleased with himself. Sometimes, he thought as rain began to spit from the low sky, sometimes you just have to make 'breaks' happen.

For the second time that week, he followed directions which had been given to him by the landlord of the Three Horseshoes. On the previous occasion he had been with

Hennessey. This time he was alone. On the previous occasion he had turned right at the end of the line of cottages and had walked up Scrivener's Folly to the home of Nancy Braithwaite, this time he turned left. The road to Five Oaks Farm revealed itself to be an unsurfaced track, not dissimilar to Scrivener's Folly, but wider, and deeply rutted, clearly having had tractors and other large vehicles driven over it for many years. Yellich was suddenly mindful of a story he had once read, set in Africa, in which a road had to be ploughed in order to make it passable to motor vehicles. The explanation which was forthcoming was that in the rainy season, the twin ruts in the road became so deep that the vehicle's bottom touched the surface between the ruts. When that happened, the road had to be ploughed level and the whole process started again. He bent down and tucked his trouser bottoms into his socks. He doubted that this road would ever need ploughing, but the ruts did indeed appear to be deep, making passage of anything less than a four-wheel drive difficult in the extreme. He walked on down the centre of the road, black winter hawthorn to his left and right, crows cawing in naked trees which stood beyond the hawthorn. It was at times like this that he knew why he was happy to be a suburban dweller, obtaining his food from the shelves of a supermarket. He was under no illusions about the nature of life in the country: it was harsh and brutal.

He reached the gate at the entrance to Five Oaks Farm, which stood to the right of the track and, like the gate at the entrance to the Manor House which he had first seen on the Thursday of that week, it too was rotten and broken and had been pushed to one side, where it had been allowed to remain. The track on which Yellich had been walking continued on across the fields, reaching some unknown destination.

Yellich walked up to the farmhouse of Five Oaks Farm. Across the fields, through the trees, he could make out the roofline of the Manor House. It was closer than he had thought and he saw then how close were the two houses. The Styleses and the Inngeys were indeed very close, geographically speaking, for rural-dwelling neighbours. The house itself was squat, like the Manor House, as if that had been the fashion hereabouts when the houses were built and it did indeed appear to Yellich's untrained eye, to be about the same vintage as the Manor House. There were vehicles arranged in front of the building, a tractor, a Land Rover, a trailer, just the sort of vehicles that would be arrayed in front of just that sort of building. Nothing seemed unusual, nothing out of place. Yellich 'read' the building and read 'hardworking', he read 'long hours' ... but he didn't see 'poverty', or 'struggle for survival'. There were vehicles outside which, whilst mud-bespattered, were not old and at the end of their lifespan, each window of the house had intact panes of glass, and the smoke rising vertically from the chimney spoke of a fire in the hearth and warmth within the house. He walked up to the door and rapped on the heavy metal knocker.

There was no answer.

He knocked again, hearing the echo of the knocking from within the house.

'Aye?' The voice came from behind him. Directly behind him. Yellich spun round. Arthur Styles stood there, broken 12-bore shotgun hanging over his right forearm; he pulled on a pipe of strong-smelling tobacco.

'Where did you come from?' Yellich asked before he realized he was speaking.

'Followed you up the lane.'

'I never noticed you.'

'I was there, behind you.'

'How far behind?'

'Far enough and close enough.' Styles avoided eye contact. 'So, what do you want?'

'Police.'

'I know ... I remember you from earlier in the week.' He nodded to the Manor House. 'I saw you at yon house ... with the other coppers ... I spoke to the old guy.'

'Mr Hennessey.'

'I don't remember his name. So, what do you want?' There was menace in his voice.

Yellich felt a twinge of fear. He felt isolated ... alone ... he yearned for a partner, another officer.

'We were just following up—'

'We were not doing anything.' Styles cut him short. 'We were alone in our car when "we" came to the village and "we" had a lonely walk round the green, then "we" went into the pub, where "we" asked directions to my house.' He plunged his hand into his jacket and pulled out a mobile. 'I have one of these fancy gadgets. I was told you were coming, so I waited for you. You didn't see me ... not until I wanted you to see me.'

Yellich too carried a mobile phone. He didn't telegraph the fact. He realized then that his mobile might be very useful indeed ... Best, he thought, best to keep it hidden.

'So forget "we" ... tell me what you want.'

'Information.'

'We all want that. What information?'

'Any information at all about the murder of the Inngeys and their maid Nancy Braithwaite.'

'Ex-maid.'

'All right, ex-maid, but she worked for them, she was connected to them and she died in the same way ... might even have been tortured before her neck was broken.' Yellich watched Styles's face and saw his lips curl briefly and almost imperceptibly into a sneer. A chill shot down his spine.

'You shouldn't have seen that.'

'Seen what?'

'Seen me smile.' Styles snapped the barrels of the shotgun against the stock and levelled them at Yellich's stomach. 'Or I shouldn't have smiled.'

'Careful ... you're committing a serious offence.'

'One more won't matter.' Styles's manner was calm, collected. 'Stay still, Mr Policeman, and don't underestimate a twelve-bore. Two inches between the barrels and your coat ... at this range it will blow you in half, and nobody will turn a hair when they hear the sound ... just old Arthur Styles potting crows.' Then he called, 'All right!'

The door of the house opened. A woman came out; she was followed by two young men, both larger and, it seemed, stronger and heavier than Yellich. One of the men felt in Yellich's pockets until he found the mobile phone. He held it up like a trophy.

'Don't press it,' Arthur Styles snarled, 'they can trace calls to their point of origin ... depends which satellite dish it bounces off.'

'Yes ... I told you that, Dad, remember,' the man protested.

'Don't answer me back. Find his car keys.'

The woman – Yellich presumed it was Arthur Styles's wife – searched his pockets and extracted his car keys. She had a pinched face and the same humourless attitude as her husband. She held up the keys.

'Give them to him.' Styles nodded to the

second young man. Yellich glanced at him. The man's eyes showed fear, as if he was out of his depth, and deeply distressed about what he was part of, but he did as he was told with unquestioning obedience, pocketing the keys as they were given to him. 'And the mobile phone.' The man looked at the second young man. 'Get rid of the car and the mobile tonight.'

'How, Dad?'

'Put the mobile in the car, drive it out somewhere ... make sure you wear gloves ... and then torch it. You follow him in the Land Rover, Prentice.'

'Right.' The first young man spoke with the same grim attitude as his father. He also had the same coldness about the eyes.

'Make sure it's done right, then bring him back.'

'Right, Dad.'

Styles prodded Yellich with the barrels of the shotgun. 'In the house, you.'

SUNDAY, 08.10 HOURS

Hennessey groaned in despair and disbelief. He lay with Louise D'Acre, on his side, his arms round her, holding her back pressed

267

up against his chest. 'Is that yours or mine?'

'It's not mine,' Louise D'Acre responded sleepily, 'mine's downstairs in the kitchen ... in my bag. If they want me out of hours, they use the land line.'

Hennessey unravelled his arms and rolled over on to his other side and walked to where he had dropped his clothes over the wicker chair which stood in the corner of Louise D'Acre's bedroom. He knew it could only mean one thing. He felt among his clothes and, finding his mobile phone, extracted it and held it to his ear. 'Hennessey,' he said softly and listened.

Louise D'Acre, too, lying still, but listening intently, knew that the plans that she had had for that day, just she and he, until her children were returned, were going to have to be remade ... and that the new plans would not involve George Hennessey.

'All right,' Hennessey said, 'I'm coming in.' He switched off the mobile. 'I'm sorry...'

'It's OK.' She turned on her back as he approached her and knelt beside her side of the bed. 'Trouble...? Well, it could only be trouble.'

'Yellich's missing...' Hennessey paused. He rested a fleshy hand on her smooth shoulder. 'He knew better ... going by himself ... he signed out yesterday, just after four p.m. going out to Long Hundred.'

'That's where the woman was found in her cottage.'

'Yes ... and other things besides.'

'Just to Long Hundred? No address?'

'No ... his wife phoned when he didn't return home ... he always phones her to let her know if he's going to be late. No phone call and no Somerled Yellich.'

'Oh ... she must be frantic. Poor woman.'

'Sent a car out to the village, couldn't find Yellich's car, then later the fire service attended a burning car ten miles from the village ... out near Pocklington ... turns out it was Yellich's car ... but no Yellich.'

'Oh...'

'So, they've got all available personnel doing everything but take the village apart and they've got the helicopter scanning the area from the air ... so I have to go in ... I'm sorry.'

'No–' she took his hand – 'don't worry ... of course you have to go in, the children go away for the weekend once every three weeks ... and this year it's their father's turn to have them for Christmas and the New

Year ... so don't worry.' She levered herself out of bed and made a long, slender arm for her robe. 'You get washed and dressed, you're not leaving this house on a day like this without a cooked breakfast and a bucket of tea inside you.'

'You'll only break your wrist.' Samantha Hewlett spoke calmly. 'Don't you think I've tried?'

Yellich relaxed. She was correct, he saw that. The chain round his wrist was too strong, too firmly attached to the wall. 'What place is this?'

Samantha Hewlett smiled.

'Glad you think it's funny.' He looked around him. It seemed to him that they were in a derelict house. The windows were intact, but there were no furnishings.

'You sound like a lost yachtsman. I used to sail off the West Coast of Scotland ... I was on a beach one day and another yacht came close inshore and hailed us, "What place is this?" I thought: My heavens, they really do say that. You read about lost ships, in the days of sail, coming close in to shore and asking where they are ... never thought I'd hear it.'

'You're calm, I must say.'

'Well, tell me what to do and I'll do it.' She too was attached to the skirting board by a length of chain which was attached to her wrists. She also had a length of chain holding her ankles together. Clearly, Yellich deduced, her abductors knew of her kick-boxing skills.

'So it was Styles all along.' Yellich relaxed against the wall.

'Yep ... he's mad. I remember that family when I was growing up in the village. They were convinced that the Inngeys had a hoard of treasure. I don't know what they thought it was going to be ... a chest full of pieces of eight and Spanish doubloons ... his obsession got the better of him.'

'He abducted them?'

'Yes.'

'When did you find out about this?'

'Friday night when they brought me here ... him and his wife ... they're as mad as each other. They want to be the top family in Long Hundred – with the Inngeys out of the way and with the Inngeys' pot of gold, they can be ... that's their thinking. Their family is as old as the Inngeys ... always played second fiddle to them ... got to hear about

271

the hidden loot ... generation ago ... now they believe I know of it, so no food for me until I tell them where it is. Anyway, just because nothing goes in, it doesn't mean it stops coming out, so sorry about the smell.'

Yellich grunted his understanding. He felt that he too would soon contribute.

'They burst into my house with a shotgun, couldn't kick-box my way round that. So how did you get here?'

Yellich told her. In the distance a train rumbled past. Heavy sound, slow-moving and this was Sunday ... a goods train, single goods ... coal for the power stations ... possibly.

'It's too remote to shout for help.' She paused. 'So no one knows where you are. Great!'

'It's a mistake I won't make again.'

'Oh, you're right there,' Samantha Hewlett snorted, 'because you won't get the opportunity. Do you think you're getting out of this alive? Do you think being a cop will protect you? It doesn't mean anything to Styles, nor to his mad wife, nor to his two mad sons ... Prentice and Leif ... particularly Prentice. Leif is soft.'

'Leif...?'

'Old Viking name ... lots of Norse blood in Yorkshire and Norse names.'

'I know.'

'Anyway, they have tortured and murdered five people already. I'm for the starvation treatment ... you ... as soon as they dig a hole in the ground, a good six feet down ... this is the country and they have all the time in the world ... and where this place is I don't know, but what I can tell you is that it's an awful long way from Long Hundred. There's no railway line anywhere near the village and the richest thing about this is that there's no treasure ... Styles is chasing a rainbow.'

Yellich smiled.

'Ha ... *now* who's got something to smile about? I am glad that you think this is funny.'

'It does, actually.'

'What does?'

'The treasure ... it does exist.'

'What?'

'Were you being truthful when you told us you only pretended to look for the treasure when you and Harold Inngey searched the old house? You took one end of the attic and he the other?'

'Yes, of course I was.'

'Well, it seems that you were sitting a few feet from it, just twiddling your thumbs when you were within arm's reach of a fortune.'

Samantha Hewlett's jaw dropped. 'Oh, what I could have had.'

'Apart from the fact that it would have saved the lives of the Inngeys and Nancy Braithwaite if the treasure had been found and was safely in the hands of its rightful owners ... apart from that, what you could have had.' Yellich was irritated by her selfishness.

'What is it ... what sort of treasure?'

'Art in the main ... small canvases ... some silver, I think ... some gold items ... but mainly art.'

Hennessey turned into Long Hundred and parked his car behind a police minibus. He scanned the village: police officers, some with dogs, seemed to him to be everywhere, knocking on doors, searching property. He was approached by a uniformed sergeant.

'Nothing yet, sir, nobody seems to have seen him.'

'Dogs pick up anything?'

'No, sir, not in this rain, and it's nearly twenty-four hours since he went missing, the rain will have taken his scent from the air ... that's where you leave your scent, in the air, not on the ground, even though dogs appear to sniff the ground.'

'I see.' Hennessey shook his head in exasperation. 'I don't believe that nobody saw anything, not in a village like this ... people do see things ... his car must have been parked here ... it must have been driven away.'

'Folk are co-operating ... letting us search their cottages ... but they seem frightened.'

'This village holds the key.' Hennessey glanced about him. 'Here ... somewhere ... something ... somebody ... it all links.'

'Yes, sir.'

'The Inngeys ... Nancy Braithwaite ... Samantha Hewlett ... and now Yellich. This place is like a black hole, people just disappear here ... . some are found ... dead.'

'There's nothing you can do, sir,' the sergeant said softly. 'Leave this to us. If he's in the village, we'll find him.'

Later that night Sara Yellich lay in bed listening to rain patter against the window.

She couldn't sleep. She thought of her husband somewhere out there ... in this weather. Jeremy was subdued, as if he had picked up his mother's anxiety. She thought about the problems she had caused ... the times she had refused him, not many, but there had been times ... too tired she had said. If he returns safely ... if ... then and for the rest of her life.

Later that night George Hennessey sat in his chair. He and Oscar had taken their walk and now Oscar sat in the corner, away from Hennessey, as if receptive to Hennessey's anxiety. By 10 p.m., not being able to settle to anything, Hennessey decided to retire for the night; there was just nothing else to do, though sleep evaded him until the dead hours.

Later that night, Samantha Hewlett shivered and said, 'What's your Christian name? I never thought of cops having Christian names.'

Yellich told her.

'What is it?'

'Gaelic.'

'S.O.R.L.E.Y.?'

'No, S.O.M.E.R.L.E.D. but it's pronounced "Sorley".'

MONDAY, 08.30 HOURS – 09.30 HOURS

Hennessey looked at Harold Inngey – the irate Harold Inngey – then at his well-dressed solicitor, Ms Pinder. She too seemed irate. 'Our action was justified, Mr Inngey ... Ms Hewlett had been abducted, a van was seen outside her house, you are known to be an associate...'

'Ex...' he snarled, 'very ex.'

'An ex-associate. So we put the door in. Any police force would have done the same ... and she is still missing, and so is my sergeant.'

'But you didn't leave a constable on the door and once you left, it was open house to all the felons on the estate ... We ... I came back to an empty house, anything of value had been taken, the rest was ransacked.'

'But we accept your alibi ... that you and Miss Josephine Pinder–' he nodded at the youthful solicitor – 'spent the weekend together. I also note that Ms Pinder is now here in a personal, not official, capacity.' Hennessey paused. 'But this may be of some compensation to you.' He took a piece of paper from his pocket and slid it across the desk top towards Harold Inngey.

'What is it?'

'A note from a friend of mine who works at Wright's the auctioneers and valuers ... good firm...'

'Yes. I know of them.'

'Well, I asked him to value the contents of the chest ... we needed to know its value for our report. He phoned this morning with his findings...'

'Ten million pounds!' Inngey was incredulous. Josephine Pinder slid her hand into his as she gaped at the piece of paper.

'Yes. That's what they said. Apparently it was mostly of only semi-value, not real top-flight treasure at all, but what had upped the value is something that sounded like a "tishun", whatever one of those is.'

'A *Titian*!' Josephine Pinder gasped, and gripped Harold Inngey's hand.

'I am sorry, my mind was elsewhere this morning. I am still worried about my sergeant.'

'Harold ... you are worth ten million pounds.' Josephine Pinder leaned over and hugged him. 'You own Edgefield House as well now. If you demolish it and sell the land for development...'

'Well, twice that at least.' Hennessey tapped the paper on the edge of the desk.

'Suspicion is largely lifted from you, Mr Inngey ... Lord Inngey ... but only largely. I would appreciate it if you would remain in York, where we can contact you if need be.'

'My house.' Josephine Pinder beamed with pride. 'He'll be at my house.' She gave an address within the walls. 'Just a few minutes' walk from here.'

Samantha Hewlett and Somerled Yellich started at the sound of the Land Rover approaching the building and then stopping.

'Reckon they've dug the hole.' Samantha Hewlett pushed herself up into a sitting position. 'I want you to tell them the treasure is in the hands of the police ... I don't want this agony prolonged ... there might be room in the hole for both of us.'

Yellich glanced at her. Even then, she could muster some dry humour.

The door of the building opened. Heavy boots tramped across bare floorboards. The door of the room which they were in was pushed open. A well-built young man stood in the door frame.

'Leif!' Samantha Hewlett looked at the man. 'Never thought it would be you ... your brother, yes ... but not you.'

'I'm done with all this.' Leif Styles looked pale. 'I didn't like it from day one ... but my dad, my older brother ... I went along, but no more.' He produced a bunch of keys from his pocket, knelt and undid the padlocks holding Samantha Hewlett to the wall, though her feet remained shackled. 'It was Prentice what done it ... broke their necks with his bare hands ... he and Dad just wouldn't believe there was no treasure ... kept them alive ... in the end they just couldn't let them live. Nancy Braithwaite ... well, plastic bag over her head ... taking it off, putting it back on again ... her heart gave out. If she'd known owt about treasure, she would have said so.' He looked at Yellich. 'Sorry about your head.'

Yellich nodded. 'Don't worry about it ... we both had a shotgun pointing at us.'

'Aye ... well, I didn't want thee to arrest me. These keys fit the padlock.'

Yellich remained silent. He knew that by doing this, Leif Styles had done himself a favour, a huge favour by doing what he was doing, but his arrest was still inevitable. 'You've got an hour ... they are coming for you in an hour ... you've got time. Follow the track from the cottage to the road, turn left, they'll be coming from the opposite direction ... just quarter of a mile ... you'll come to South Fryston, there's a phone box there outside the Fleece.'

He dropped the bunch of keys at Samantha Hewlett's feet, turned, walked out of the room, out of the building, and was heard to drive slowly away.